Conflicted

Samantha Snyman

Published by Samantha Snyman, 2024.

CONFLICTED

First edition. October 24, 2024.

ISBN: 979-8227425607

Written by Samantha Snyman.

We loved with a love that was more than love ~ Edgar Allen Poe

Chapter 1

A theory exists that throughout our lifetime, we will have two or even three great loves and each of these will help shape us into the person we will ultimately become. They will be unique and we will learn different lessons from them. I don't know whether this is true or not, but I do know that I was fortunate enough to have had three of them during my life's journey and they were epic. Looking back, I guess I have learned a few valuable lessons, but most importantly, I experienced happiness and love in so many unexpected and different ways that it made all the heartbreak worth it.

In my junior year in high school, my best friend, Bev and I were on our way to Massachusetts. Her grandma lived there, in a small house near the beach.

"Are you girls sure you packed everything? You'll be staying for a week and it's a long drive. I can't simply turn around and come home if you've forgotten something."

My mom was driving us and boy was she over-protective. She was sweet though, and not the kind of person you could stay mad at.

"Yes, mom. We're sure." I rolled my eyes and smiled at her. My mom had a heart of gold and we had the best relationship. I knew how blessed I was to have her as my mother. Bev, on the other hand, wasn't as close to hers, but she had her grandma whom she adored.

It was a blast visiting the octogenarian. I loved the beach, the people, the town and the serenity I felt when I sat on the porch at the end of a day, staring at the magical sunset which painted the ocean gold. I've always had a special love for the ocean. I was mesmerized by the sound of the waves, the feeling of the wet sand between my toes and the exquisite beauty of every unique wave.

When we finally pulled up in front of Aunt Lillian's house, I got out of the car and took it all in. The smell of the ocean, the wind through my hair and the sound of the waves. When I opened my eyes, I caught my mom smiling at me.

"You really do love the ocean, Hannah." I gave her a hug and thanked her for driving us.

"I'm sure Granny would like to see you, Aunt Addy." I could see the excitement in Bev's eyes as she took her suitcase out of the trunk. We made our way inside where Aunt Lillian was busy making coffee.

"My beautiful girls have arrived!"

Mom looked at me with the biggest smile on her face and I knew in that instant how proud of me she was. That particular smile always appeared whenever anyone said something good about me or I'd achieved some kind of success.

Bev and I took our luggage to our rooms and left the grown ups to talk. My room was decorated in lavenders and greys. It was small and cozy and had the most beautiful view of the ocean.

"You know we simply have to go out a bit this week. I would really like to introduce you to some of my friends," Bev said from the doorway.

Each time we came to Massachusetts, I would spend most of my time at the beach. I never went out with Bev or made new friends, but this time I'd promised Mom I would make an effort to be more spontaneous. "Sure Bev. Anything for you." She squealed and jumped on me and we both landed on the floor in a tangle of arms and legs.

All my life, I've never liked being the centre of attention. I've always worn neutral coloured clothing and tied my hair in an uninspired ponytail. Bev was the complete opposite. She loved bright colours and was always experimenting with new hairstyles. She was gorgeous. Sometimes, I envied her. Her confidence and spontaneous personality made it easy for her to get along with most people. Bev always chose to hang out with boys. She always said that girls were too much drama.

"Let's go say goodbye to my mom." I always felt sad when she had to leave and Bev knew this.

"Don't worry, Hannah. I'll take care of you." Bev smiled at me and I felt better. Even though I was older by five months, she was mostly the more mature one.

We walked into the kitchen just as my mom was giving Aunt Lillian a hug. "Please call me if you need anything or if the girls give you any trouble." She winked at me.

Aunt Lillian laughed and put her arm around Bev's shoulders. "They are total angels. You have nothing to worry about."

I gave my mom a hug and said in a very quiet voice: "I'll miss you Mom. Please drive safely." She must've seen the tears in my eyes, because she took my face in her hands and kissed my forehead.

"You'll have so much fun my baby. I love you." I decided to give Bev and Aunt Lillian time to catch up and changed into my bathing suit; a black one piece, simple and comfortable. I knew Bev would give me a speech about rather wearing a bikini. I threw on a t-shirt and shorts, and left the house.

"I'm going to dip my toes in the ocean," I said as I walked past Aunt Lillian and Bev who were drinking coffee in the kitchen.

"I know what you're wearing under that t-shirt! We'll talk about that later!" I almost ran when I heard that. Aunt Lillian must've seen this, because she started laughing loudly. I liked feeling comfortable in my clothes. I never really cared what people thought about me. Although I had to admit that the bathing suit was in need of a replacement; it didn't really fit all that well anymore.

This was my favourite part, when I could curl my toes in the sand and allow the saltwater to wash over my feet. It was like greeting an old friend who'd been away for a long time. I closed my eyes and smiled. Gratitude overwhelmed me. I sat down in the sand and stared at the ocean. This was my happy place. I was so focused on the beauty in front of me that I didn't notice that someone was approaching me.

"Hi there." Startled, I looked up into the deepest blue eyes I've ever seen. For a moment, I was paralyzed. "Are you from out of town?" He sat down beside me and I forced myself to speak.

"Hi... yes, I'm actually from Boston." My voice sounded unsteady, and I cleared my throat before continuing, "I'm Hannah."

For a few heartbeats, he simply looked at me. "I'm Elijah. Nice to meet you."

I couldn't stop staring at his eyes. It reminded me of the ocean. "Likewise." Suddenly I was very aware of how small my bathing suit was and I felt uncomfortable. I jumped up, put my t-shirt and shorts back on and started walking away. "I have to go, see you around!" I didn't look back, even as I heard him call my name. I was too embarrassed; I just kept on walking.

Back home, Bev was lying on my bed. "Why do you look so flustered?" She sat up and examined me from head to toe.

I braced myself. "I met a boy." She squealed and an angry look marred her features. "Wearing that? Seriously, Hannah. When will you start listening to me? You have such nice clothes, but all you wear are t-shirts and shorts."

I rolled my eyes, arguing would be pointless. "I'm going to take a shower and curl up with a nice book."

She got up and grabbed me by the arm. "We are going out. Go shower and I'll put together an outfit for you."

I began to protest, but she held up her hand, and I sighed. "Fine! But nothing too flashy, please. Practice some restraint!"

Bev had chosen a pair of my skinny jeans and a yellow strapless top which boasted tiny white butterflies. The top obviously belonged to her. She winked at me and continued applying her make-up.

"I'll wear the clothes you picked out for me, but I'm not wearing any make-up, and my hair stays in a ponytail."

Bev turned around and took my hands. "Please lose the ponytail!"

I hated the fact that I could hardly ever say no to her. "Fine." She smiled and turned back towards the mirror.

"Let your hair down. Literally and figuratively." We both laughed.

I looked at myself in the mirror. I could barely recognize myself. "Wow, I look different."

Bev smiled proudly. "Different in a good way, my friend. Although, I don't like the fact that your boobs are bigger than mine." Bev looked genuinely disappointed. I struggled to find the right words. Sometimes she could be so childish.

"You make up for it in so many other ways, Bev."

And just like that, she was happy again. "Let's go, sexy nerd!"

I took a deep breath and followed her. "We're going out Aunt Lillian. Please pray for me."

Aunt Lillian laughed. "Don't be back too late girls!"

We walked in silence for a while before Bev stopped and turned towards me. She had a serious expression on her face. "You'll interact, you'll have fun and you won't pass any judgment. Kapish?" I almost burst out laughing, but instead I nodded in agreement.

The pub Bev finally chose sported arcade games, pool tables, comfortable chairs and a heavy oak bar. The music wasn't too loud and the establishment exuded a chill vibe. I liked it. A group of boys were sitting at a table in the back. One of them spotted us and came over. He picked Bev up in his arms and twirled her around.

"How have you been hot stuff? And who's you friend?"

A familiar voice came from behind me. "This is Hannah from Boston." I turned around and looked right into the same pair of deep blue eyes. And yet again, I was lost for words. Bev put her arm around my neck.

"So, Elijah is the boy from the beach?" Bev asked.

I could feel my cheeks getting warm and tried to sound as casual as I could. "Yeah. We met earlier today." Bev took the other boy's hand and led him to the table where the others were waiting. "Come along, Hannah. Meet the rest of the boys."

I followed her, but Elijah pulled me back gently and whispered in my ear. "You're cute when you blush." Warmth suffused my face. I was annoyed with myself, but joined Bev and the guys anyway. "Hi everyone. I'm Hannah," I introduced myself. They were Don, Jeremiah, Josh, Drake and Levi. "It's going to take a while to remember your names," I said, smiling. Then I looked at Elijah. His name I wouldn't forget. We had loads of fun talking, laughing and playing pool. I liked all of them, but Drake kept flirting with me and he was coming on pretty strongly. I wanted to tell him to stop, but didn't want to spoil everyone else's fun.

"Want to take a walk?" Elijah asked. It was as if he could sense that I needed help. I looked at him and nodded. "He was coming on way too strong," he said, laughing.

"I'm really not used to it. Boys usually don't notice me at all." I immediately regretted the sudden confession. It sounded like I pitied myself.

Elijah looked at me suspiciously. "Yeah, right. I find it hard to believe that boys aren't interested in you at all." He certainly had a way with words, judging by the amount of blushing I was doing. "Look, Hannah, I don't like to beat around the bush. I like you. And I would like to get to know you better."

I was mesmerized by his words, his eyes, his smell and his confidence. I was still searching for the right words to say when he put his hand out and gently brushed my hair from my face. "I'm going to kiss you now." He didn't wait for a reply. He simply kissed me. And that was it. I was in love. Head over heels.

The boys walked us home later that night. Elijah and I were some way behind them. His arm was around my waist, and I felt warm and safe. Every so often, Bev would turn and look at us. I could see the approval and excitement on her face. The closer we got to home, the clearer I could hear ocean.

"Don't you just love that sound?" I asked. Elijah spun me around and kissed me.

"I do. Now even more than before." I didn't quite understand what he meant. He must've seen the confusion on my face. "Now that I know how much you love the ocean, it makes me love it more too."

I smiled and hugged him.. "Thanks for rescuing me tonight." I turned around and he pulled me back to kiss me again. We were home sooner than I wished to be.

"Enough you two!" Bev sounded just a tad jealous.

"Goodnight!" Elijah called as he turned and ran to catch up with his friends.

"Tell me everything." Bev said eagerly. We'd gone inside and were in my bedroom. Bev closed the door so as not to wake Aunt Lillian. "How was the kiss?"

I laughed, which is something I do when I get nervous. "It was hot. Like really hot."

Bev squealed and started to jump up and down. "What can I say? You're welcome, babe." Bev looked so smug and proud of herself.

"Well, I like to think that I had a little something to do with this too," I said while changing into my oversized Mikey Mouse t-shirt.

"Honey, we need to get you some real pj's," Bev said, disapproval written all over her face.

I couldn't care less. "I'm knackered. Goodnight, Bev. It was fun, thanks."

Bev never could take a hint, not even when one slapped her in the face. "So, what are we doing tomorrow?"

I didn't even have to think twice. "We are going to the beach, of course."

Bev shook her head angrily. "No, you know the ocean and I are not on friendly terms. The water is too salty and there's sand everywhere."

I could never understand how anyone could not like the ocean. "You can tan. I know you like that." I knew I had her when she didn't reply immediately.

"I guess tanning on the beach, while sipping smoothies wouldn't be the worst thing in the world. I have one condition though."

She left the room and came back ten seconds later. She threw a blue bikini onto my bed. It still had the tags on it.

"It's beautiful Bev, but I don't think I can wear this."

Bev shrugged. "Then no beach."

I covered my face with my hands. "Argghhh! Fine!"

Bev smiled and turned off the light. "Goodnight, dear friend. No reading tonight. You need your beauty sleep." Bev slipped out of the room and closed the door softly behind her.

I got under the covers, turned on the bedside lamp, opened my favourite book, The Great Gatsby and lost myself within the pages.

The next morning, I examined myself in the mirror. The bikini was a perfect fit. I couldn't believe how comfy it felt.

Bev barged into my room without knocking, as usual. "Wow! You look hot!"

I actually felt hot, which was a first. "Let's go to the beach!" I threw on a blue SpongeBob t-shirt as cover-up.

Bev shook her head and handed me a pair of sunglasses. Bev looked beautiful in her hot pink bikini. Her hair was pulled back into a high bun and loose curls were hanging down both sides of her face. She had a pink see through beach dress on over her bikini.

"We're going to the beach Granny!" she shouted as we neared the front door.

Aunt Lillian poked her head out of the kitchen. "You girls look so pretty. Please be careful and look after one another." Aunt Lillian was one of the most loving people I knew. I loved the way that she cared about everyone in her vicinity.

"Don't worry. We'll be safe. Promise," I said and waved at her. We trekked to the beach, carrying two umbrellas, beach towels, water and sunscreen. As soon as we arrived, I threw down our belongings, pulled my t-shirt off and ran into the ocean. I didn't mind the saltiness of the water, I would swim for hours if I could. Bev called me, and I felt like pretending that I hadn't heard her. True to form, I immediately felt guilty. I turned around and saw Elijah standing there. The others I had met the previous evening were also there, but my eyes were glued to Elijah. I swam back as fast as I could and walked out of the surf. All of the guys' eyes were on me, and it hit me. like a bolt of like lightning. My bikini! "Bev! Please bring me my t-shirt!" The moment the words left my lips, I knew she wouldn't do it. She wanted me to show off my body in the new bikini.

"No can do, babe! Come show these boys how hot you are!"

Defeated, I walked towards them. Elijah picked up my shirt and brought it to me. I couldn't get it on fast enough.

"For the record, you are super-hot." His voice was hoarse with repressed emotion.

It made my entire body tingle. How was it possible that this boy whom I'd literally known for day, could make me feel things I'd never felt before? "Thank you," I mumbled, knowing that he'd hear the anxiety in my voice. "Did Bev invite you?" A rhetorical question to which he nodded. I should've been angry at Bev, but looking into his eyes, I couldn't feel anything but happy. He took me in his arms and kissed me passionately. I was experiencing all these different and unfamiliar feelings to the extent that I could barely think straight.

"You're such a good kisser, Hannah. I could kiss you forever." And he did.

I was floating on cloud nine; the butterflies in my stomach fluttered frantically. I didn't want it to stop...ever.

Chapter 2

We hung out with the guys every day for the rest of the week. Elijah and I spent most of the time alone together. We would take long walks on the beach and talk for hours. And every time we kissed, it felt like the first time. I could picture myself kissing only this boy for the rest of my life. I was so in love with him. He was sincere, loyal and a straight shooter. No games. I liked that. He told me that I had the prettiest smile he'd ever seen and the fact that I wasn't even aware of the effect my beauty had on people, was making me even more attractive to him. I believed him. For the first time, I actually felt beautiful and attractive.

I decided to change my look. The ponytail took a hike and I started wearing lip gloss. This was as far as I went, because I still wanted to be me. Bev was ecstatic. She immediately gathered all her lip gloss tubes and started testing them on me.

"You have to look fabulous for our last night here. Don is having a party at his parents' beach house." I was so bummed that this would be our last night in Massachusetts, but I knew, like all other good things, this too had to come to an end.

When I got out of the shower, Bev have already picked out an outfit for me; a purple mini dress, simple, yet pretty. "I actually like this, thanks Bev." She smiled and took a bow. I busted out laughing. I wore my hair in a loose braid and put on a very light pink lip gloss. Bev wore a white mini skirt and blue crop top. Her hair was loose and curly. She looked gorgeous as always.

"Let's have dinner before we go to the party," Bev suggested.

I was surprised that she'd want to eat. The party had already started and I knew Bev hated to be late, but I happily obliged. Aunt Lillian had made pasta with a green salad on the side. It was delicious. "You truly are one of the best cooks I know, Aunt Lillian." She smiled and I could tell she appreciated the compliment.

"Yes, thanks Granny. The food was delicious, as always." Bev got up and washed her hands. "Come on, Hannah. It's time to go."

I was in a hurry to see Elijah again, but I felt guilty for leaving Aunt Lillian to do the washing up on her own. "Let's first do the dishes. You're Gran's already done the cooking by herself." I could see that Bev was annoyed, but I carried on clearing the table.

"Thank you, girls. I am kind of tired. Come home at a decent hour, won't you?"

Bev threw the dishes in the dishwasher so quickly, I was afraid she might break something. "Sure, no problem, Gran. Have a good evening." She gave me a wicked look and I knew I had to hurry up.

There were a lot of unfamiliar faces at the party. I searched for the only one I really wanted to see, but could not find him. Bev had already disappeared into the crowd. I decided to stand on the porch and look at the ocean. I wanted to soak up as much of it as I could before leaving. Suddenly, I felt his arms around me and I smiled.

"There you are." I turned around at the unfamiliar voice. I was about to speak when Elijah appeared and punched the guy in the face. I stepped in between them and took Elijah's hand. "Let's just go."

He glared at the guy before he turned his gaze on me. "Yes, let's take a walk," he said. We struggled through the crowd and left the house behind. He stopped, looked at me, picked me up and twirled me around. "You look amazing. So damn hot."

I blushed. "You're not so bad yourself." He was wearing denim jeans and a blue t-shirt that really brought out the colour of his gorgeous eyes. "You know, I really could stare into your eyes all day. It reminds me of the ocean." He pulled me closer and kissed me so passionately I thought I would faint. My whole body was weak. I held onto him for dear life.

"I'm leaving tomorrow. Would you like to stay in touch?" He looked at me and smiled.

"Of course I would."

We spent the evening on the beach, talking about our dreams and hopes for the future. The conversation was effortless; Elijah was easy to be around. As we walked home later that evening, I asked him if he wanted my number. He took out his phone and handed it to me. He had a picture of a dog as his screensaver. I was curious, but didn't ask. I saved my number and gave the phone back. When we reached the house, he tenderly took my face in his hands and kissed me.

"I'm really going to miss you, Hannah. I'm so glad we met. Please take care of yourself." I could feel tears burning behind my eyelids, but I managed to keep them at bay.

"You too. I had a great time. Thank you." I gave him a hug and went inside. I walked to my room, closed the door, fell on the bed and cried like I never had before. From sheer exhaustion, I fell asleep just as the sky was lightening. I hadn't even known this boy that long, but it felt like I was leaving a piece of my heart behind. Little did I know that it was exactly what was happening.

Back at home, I waited anxiously to hear from him. There were no calls, no texts, nothing. His silence was painful and unexpected. It just never crossed my mind that he wouldn't contact me. I tried to bury my sadness, but my mom could see right through me. To her I was an open book. She took the time to console me.

"Your future will be filled with happiness and love my baby, this I can promise you. Don't lose hope."

I laid my head in her lap and cried myself to sleep. I was dreading going back to school, which was in three days' time. It was my last semester of junior year and I decided to make the best of it. I'd leave the past behind me and move into the future with a positive attitude.

"That would look great on you babe!" Bev had persuaded me to go shopping. According to her, I needed new clothes. She was convinced that retail therapy would heal my broken heart. She held out a pair of skinny jeans and a black crop top. I was still considering the ensemble when she held up a t-shirt dress with the word Nerd printed across the chest. It was exactly my kind of dress.

"I love it!" I took the dress from her and disappeared into the fitting room.

"You look great," Bev said peeking through the curtain.

"Thanks for caring so much about me, Bev."

"Always," she said as she smiled at me.

We went home with no less than five shopping bags that day and wonder of wonders, I'd actually enjoyed it. I was feeling much better and ready to start a new chapter of my life. Yes, my heart was still broken and I still missed Elijah and his ocean blue eyes, but I was determined to move on. I'd cherish the moments we had spent together, but I had to let him go. He would never occupy a space in my heart again.

My first day back at school was the same as any other. Mom made waffles, pancakes and cappuccino. "Good morning, baby. You look fabulous." I was wearing my new t-shirt dress and sneakers. My hair was frizzy and tied in a high ponytail.

"Thanks, Mom. I just hope Bev doesn't give me a hard time about the ponytail again." Mom laughed and handed me a plate. "Thanks, everything looks delicious." She nodded before picking up her bag and files from the counter.

"Have a good first day back, honey." She kissed my forehead and headed out. I was so proud of her. She's the most hard-working person I knew. Helping others has always been her passion, which is why her profession suited her like a glove. She's a trauma counsellor. People loved her, because her aura exuded peace and comfort.

My phone rang. It was Bev. "Where are you?! We're going to be late!"

I rolled my eyes and downed the rest of my cappuccino quickly. "On my way!"

I looked around in the classroom. Everything still looked the same, but I'd changed. I felt like I didn't belong.

"This seat taken?" Alex asked.

He'd moved to Boston two years ago and we've been in the same class since then, although we never really talked to each other. "No, it's not." I smiled at him.

He sat down and turned to me. "How are you, Hannah? You look different."

I was caught off guard. Why would Alex talk to me. Especially now. And then it hit me. Bev! "Did Bev ask you to come and talk to me?" The anger in my voice was clear as crystal and I saw him back up a little.

"No. Why would she? Are you okay?"

The confusion on his face was genuine.

I was mortified. "OMG, I'm so sorry. I thought.... never mind. I'm just sorry." Our teacher, Mr. Clint walked in. I wasn't his biggest fan, but in that moment, I was grateful. He'd saved me from further embarrassment. For the rest of the day, I tried to avoid Alex.

"What did you and Alex talk about earlier?" Bev had that look in her eyes. A plan was brewing in her pretty little head.

"Please don't do anything. I just want to finish this year without any more heartache."

Bev took my hand in hers and cleared her throat; she was serious. "Babe, all of the boys won't break your heart. Besides, who says you can't be friends with Alex?"

That actually made sense to me. It would be nice to have more than one friend. "That's actually great advice, Bev. Thanks." During lunchtime, I sat alone in the cafeteria and my mind took me to the ocean, which had once upon a time been my happy place. Now, it was tainted by the bitterness of unrequited love.

I wondered whether I'd ever go back to Massachusetts. I honestly didn't know.

Alex entered the cafeteria and I decided to be brave and make a new friend. I approached him and we started talking. Being in his presence was super easy and comfortable. I simply knew that it would be the beginning of a beautiful friendship. We began to spend a lot of time together at school and at home.

He surprised me one day by taking me to the aquarium. As expected, Bev became jealous of all the time I was spending with Alex. Our friendship was vastly different from the one I had with Bev. Alex and I could talk for hours about any and everything. I'd even told him about Elijah.

"Why are you spending more time with Alex than with me. Is he your new bestie now? Have I been replaced?" Bev asked late one afternoon. Anger was building like vicious storm clouds on her face. This side of Bev freaked me out. This was definitely not normal behaviour. The fact that this was all about me, made it weirder.

"Bev, you know no one can ever take your place in my heart. You have nothing to worry about."

She shrugged and said smugly: "Yeah, I'm special like that." And we both laughed out loud.

Later, that same afternoon, I had a study date with Alex at his house. He was home alone. His parents travelled a lot for work. I felt so sorry for him. I know how lonely I would've been had I been in his shoes.

"Coffee, tea, me?" Alex had a way of making me laugh. It was one of the many things I liked about him.

"Coffee, thanks." I sat down on the carpet in the lounge and took out my books. "You know, I've thought about it a lot and I've decided that I would like to go back to Massachusetts. I won't let a boy come between me and the ocean. Does that sound weird?"

Alex came in with my coffee and some cookies. "No, I understand and agree with you 100%. Don't let anyone ever take your happiness, or in your case, your happy place, away from you." He had a way with words. I always felt better when I was with him.

"You're such a great friend, Alex." He looked at me, leaned over and kissed me. It happened so fast. I pulled away quickly. "I.... I don't want to ruin our friendship." The kiss had been breath-taking and I wanted to kiss him again, but our friendship was too valuable.

And then Alex said something that changed everything. He leaned forward and whispered in my ear. "We can be friends with benefits." I didn't think twice. I kissed him. It felt so good, so safe, and oh so hot. I pushed him down on the floor and sat on top of him. We kissed as if the earth was going to implode. This was different, exciting and I really enjoyed it.

I've never kept secrets from Bev before, but I knew Alex was right. Telling people, even just one person, could really complicate things and ruin our friendship. Besides, part of the exhilaration was the fact that we were keeping this a secret from everyone. It was a whole new experience. I grew to love Alex; he was a superb friend and the fact that he was a really good kisser, didn't hurt. I never thought that a friendship which included make out sessions could work, but it did for us.

We hung out almost every day and made out occasionally. Alex said that balance was key. Friends first and benefits later. One afternoon, I was reading on his bed while he was showering. I was tired and my eyelids were drooping. He sauntered into the room with a towel wrapped around his waist. His hair was wet, his abs, his arms... oh boy. How had I never noticed how hot he was before. He walked toward me and opened the drawer next to his bed.

"Are you okay?" I looked up into his blue-grey eyes. His lips beckoned me and I struggled to find the words to answer him. Instead, I pulled him down on top of me and kissed him passionately. Things got so intense between us, I could feel my body temperature rising. He must've noticed, because he started to get up, but I pulled him back.

"Do you have protection?" I knew this was it. I wanted to do it with him. I was ready.

He looked at me suddenly confused. "I thought you wanted to wait for the right one?"

I smiled and stroked his face with the back of my hand. "Alex, you are my friend. I trust you. I feel safe with you. I want you to be the one." He smiled and that was it, the night I lost my virginity. He was so considerate and gentle. It was perfect.

"Can I draw you a bath?" he asked as I lay in his arm.

"Yes please. You can join if you feel like it or would that be overstepping my bounds and running into dangerous territory?" I asked.

He laughed and rolled his body on top of me. "No, that would be great, but first...."

It's true that time flies when you're having fun. Prom was right around the corner and Bev and I had decided to go together. She picked out both our dresses. Mine was white and hers gold. I didn't really want to go, but she hadn't given me a choice.

I was busy doing homework in my room when my phone rang. It was an unfamiliar number.

"Hello," a voice said. I recognized it instantaneously. "How have you been, Hannah?"

I was contemplating hanging up. I was so over him and never spent a second thinking about him anymore. "What do you want Elijah?"

He was silent for a while and I felt bad for being so hostile. "Can I please explain?" he asked. I didn't say anything. "I'm sorry. I was a jerk. I'm transferring to your school next year and I wanted to clear the air between us."

This was the last thing I'd expected. I was furious. "Consider the air cleared!" I hung up and cried like a baby. I pulled myself together and headed off to Alex's.

He opened the door, took one look at my face and asked, "That bad huh? Chocolate milkshake?" He ushered me into the living room, sat me down on the sofa and disappeared into the kitchen. Three minutes later, I was lying in his lap as tears streamed down my cheeks. He stroked my hair and whispered, "Everything will be okay. I'm always here for you. And remember, you are stronger now. Just don't let him in again." I nodded, extremely grateful that Alex had been home.

I didn't hear from Elijah again, but it didn't matter. His voice once again echoed through my memories. I missed him and I hated myself for it. Bev's advice was not to be too hard on myself and that time would heal all wounds. What a cliché! Time has never healed anything, it simply makes it bearable and less visible. Wounds pertaining to the heart would always be there. I was a firm believer in that whatever was meant to be, would be. It's something we have no control over. It's destiny.

Chapter 3

"Make me pretty." Bev's eyes lit up at my words, like she'd just won the lottery.

"Finally! I've been waiting a lifetime to give you a makeover! Get ready to look absolutely drop dead gorgeous!" It was prom night and Bev had come to my house so we could get ready together. Once she was finished with my hair and make-up, she called my mom.

"Oh honey! You look beautiful!" Tears welled up in her eyes.

"Thanks, Mom. It's Bev's handiwork. You have no idea how much I've needed this. Thanks, Bev. I got up and looked at myself in the mirror. "Wow! This might sound conceited, but I do look really pretty." My mom and Bev both laughed.

My hair was styled in wavy curls. I had silver eyeshadow on, but it was barely noticeable. The perfect shade of pink lipstick completed the look. The white, satin dress Bev had picked out for me had thin straps and an open back. It accentuated my body's curves.

"You'll have to go commando, babe." Bev suggested and she was dead serious. "It's either that or everyone will see your panty line. Your choice."

I shrugged, accepting my fate. I took my underwear off. and perused myself thoroughly in the mirror, making sure that nothing untoward was showing. I wore my Mom's fine silver necklace and pearl earrings. Bev looked breath-taking in her gold, princess-style dress. Her hair was hanging loose, straight and sleek and she wore gold jewellery.

I could feel everyone's eyes on me as I entered the hall. I almost turned around, but then I saw Alex walking towards me in a black tuxedo and navy-blue shirt. He looked so handsome.

"May I have this dance pretty lady?" I gave him my hand and he led me onto the dance floor. He leaned in and whispered in my ear: "You have no idea what I want to do you right now."

I couldn't help but smile. "Why don't you take me home and show me?" I'd barely finished my sentence when he took me by the hand and walked towards the exit. He kept looking at me while we drove to his house.

"Eyes on the road," I admonished.

He laughed. "I can't help it. You look so damn gorgeous!" I couldn't believe that I'd literally left the prom within five minutes of my arrival with a boy who was at best simply a good friend. But I preferred to be with him, alone, making out. It would be way more fun than the prom, guaranteed.

We'd barely entered his house when we started making out. Our bodies were magnets, inexorably and forcefully drawn to each other. I started undressing first and he followed. The passion between us was like fireworks, jagged lightning. I was out of control and I loved every second of it. He picked me up in his arms and I wrapped my legs around his waist. We made love that night and it was like nothing I'd ever experienced before with Alex. I didn't want it to end. It just felt right.

Afterwards we lay next to each other on his bed, staring at the ceiling. "You can sleep over if you want. I don't think your mom would mind. Would that be weird for you?"

I actually liked the idea of getting into a warm bath with him and spending the night together. "I'll text her right now. She won't have a problem. She knows we are friends." I took out my phone and texted her.

"Yeah, good friends." He sounded disappointed. I turned to look at him, but he got up and got dressed. My mom replied and agreed just like we knew she would. "My mom said yes. Should we take a bath?" I looked at him, trying to gauge his feelings.

"Awesome," he said nonchalantly.

I thought I'd be relieved, but I actually felt disappointed.

I went to the bathroom and ran us a bath. "I don't have any extra clothing or underwear, Alex"

He winked at me and said rather wickedly: "You can wear my t-shirt. And as for underwear.... you don't need any."

For the first time I blushed at something he'd said. What was happening? Was I catching feelings? This was dangerous for our friendship. I shoved the questions aside. "Your wish is my command," I said as I smiled got into the bathtub. He got in behind me.

"So, will you be going to Massachusetts for break?"

Suddenly, it felt like a loaded question. "What do you think I should do?" This was something I would normally ask him, but somehow it felt different. Everything we were saying to each other sounded off kilter.

"I think that you should do what makes you happy. I know the ocean makes you happy. Guard your heart when you're there."

He was so sweet. I laid my head on his chest. "This feels so nice." He squirted body wash onto a sponge and bathed me.

"This is the best friendship I've ever had, that's for sure."

I couldn't see his face, but I knew he was smiling. He was my secret addiction and I had to get my fix on a regular basis. "Let's order pizza and watch movies. Do you have chocolates and some chips?"

He kissed my neck before whispering in my ear: "I don't want anything, but you tonight."

My heart raced as he caressed my neck. Boy, was he getting to me! "We need to eat if we're going to keep this up. I presume this is exactly what you have in mind for the evening." Alex laughed deep in his throat.

When I left Alex's house morning, I felt sad. I didn't want to be away from him and it scared me. I was falling for him and knew it would ruin our friendship. Bev hadn't asked whether I would be going to Massachusetts for break and I was contemplating bringing up the discussion with her. I really missed the beach. Even when it's cold, it's beautiful. I was also looking forward to spending some quality time with my mom.

"Hi friend! Can I even call you that anymore?" Bev asked as she stood in the doorway of my bedroom.

"What's up with the dramatics? I gave her a hug and pinched her cheek playfully. I knew she was disappointed that I'd left prom so earl without telling her.

"I'll forgive you this time. Why did you leave so early? On a different note, do you still want to come to Massachusetts with me? My brother's driving down tomorrow." Suddenly the answer seemed easy. "Of course I do, but only for a week or so. I really want to spend some time with my mom too."

She nodded and studied me intently. "Something is different about you. I just can't figure out what it is."

I was shocked and shut down for a moment. "I don't know what you mean. Come on, let's go ask my mom about Massachusetts." I succeeded in distracting her, but I knew Bev well enough to know that she wouldn't let it go. Mom said yes and offered to pick me up in a week.

"Better start packing, babe. And please, keep the oversize t-shirts to a minimum." I shrugged and threw all my clothes on the bed. I hated packing, so I left the mess behind and walked to Alex's to say goodbye.

I rang the doorbell and as soon as he opened the door, I started talking. "I'm leaving for Massachusetts tomorrow."

For a moment he stared at me before picking me up and carrying me inside. "Then we'd better make use of the time we have left." I was actually hoping we could talk, but when we kissed, all reason disappeared. We made out for almost an hour. My lips were numb, but I didn't want to stop. I started to unbutton my shirt, but he stopped me.

"You do know that I don't just want to have sex with you, right? You mean so much more to me and I don't want you to doubt that, ever." My heart was thumping wildly in my chest. I kissed him as if my life depended on it and continued undressing.

Much later, I asked, "Do you have any plans for break?"

He ran his fingers through his hair. "Yeah, I'm going to Spain to visit an old family friend."

I wondered whether this friend was a girl, but I didn't ask. "How long will you be gone?" I tried to sound normal, but I wasn't good at pretending.

He pinched my chin playfully. "I'll try to come back when you do. We can have a movie marathon. How does that sound?" I loved the idea. I suddenly felt more excited about this than the trip to Massachusetts. OMG I was in trouble. "Sounds great. So, I'd better get going. I still have to pack. Goodbye, Alex. I'll see you soon."

He grabbed my arm and pulled me in for a kiss. "Goodbye my beautiful friend. I miss you already." I walked out the door without looking back. I knew he was watching me walk away and I wouldn't have been able to resist running back for another make out session.

When I got home, Bev was busy packing my clothes. I was so happy that I hugged her. "You're the best friend ever!"

She shoved me aside. "Yeah, I know I'm awesome." She stopped packing and looked at me suspiciously. "Okay, out with it. Where have you been and what were you doing? And what the heck has happened to you? And don't even think about lying to me."

I couldn't think of a way to avoid her questions and lying wasn't an option. I sucked at that. The truth remained. I sat down next to her on the bed and sighed. "I need you to promise that you won't ever tell anyone and you won't judge." Bev loved secrets and I could see the excitement in her eyes.

"I promise. Now please tell me." I took a deep breath and tried to remember how it had all started.

"Well, Alex and I agreed to be friends with benefits." Bev jumped up and squealed. She clapped her hands and started giggling. I told her everything. Every last juicy detail. It actually felt good to share all those amazing experiences with her. "I don't think I've ever seen you speechless before, Bev. I have to record this moment." I took out my phone and took a picture.

"I'm going to need a minute to process this," she said. I got up and finished packing in silence. "So, let me get this straight. You and Alex have been making out in secret for months now. You've lost your virginity and are actually having sex with him for fun?"

I folded my purple hoodie and packed it into the suitcase. "No. You make it sound like I'm a slut or something. I only have sex with Alex and I don't quite know how to explain it. It's like this uncontrollable and magnetic pull between us. And remember we are just friends."

Bev got up and took my face in her hands. "I can't believe this. Who are you and what have you done with Hannah? You are a badass!"

Chapter 4

I was just beginning to doze off when a text from Alex woke me, asking me to meet him outside. Hastily I threw on my hoodie and boots and made my way outside to find him waiting in his car. "I brought Starbucks," he greeted me as I climbed in, turning on the heater.

"What's up? Is everything alright?" I secretly hoped he would invite me to stay over again.

"It's all good. I just realized how much I'll miss you this week," he confessed, his words making my heart skip a beat. Taking a sip of the Starbucks, I was struck by its bold flavor, much like the intensity of our moments together.

"We'll still video call, won't we? And aren't you tired of having me around all the time?" He tenderly caressed my cheek, sending a shiver down my spine with his touch. The palpable connection between us conveyed unspoken emotions.

"I can't touch you through a screen. The lack of my Hannah-fix might lead to withdrawal," he teased. I laughed, feeling anxious about our separation. Perhaps a break would clarify our feelings, as the lines between friendship and something more were starting to blur.

Hours passed in conversation and laughter until I realized dawn was approaching. "It's late; I really should get going," I reluctantly announced, torn between wanting to stay and knowing I had to leave. His kiss made me reconsider, but I summoned all of my self-control and forced myself out of the car.

The drive to Massachusetts felt oddly shorter this time. I was replaying each encounter me and Alex had together in my head, trying to figure out what exactly we shared – it sure as hell wasn't just friendship. I was scared out of my mind of losing him, which was bound to happen if we were to be a couple. If life has taught me anything, it's that nothing good ever lasted forever.

When we arrived at Aunt Lillian's house, I did my usual routine. I took a deep breath, embraced the surroundings, and soaked it all in. I was back at my happy place. I snapped a selfie with the ocean in the background and sent it to Alex. Inside the house, Aunt Lillian was baking ginger biscuits, Bev's favorite. I greeted her with a hug. "It's great to see you again, Aunt Lillian. I've missed you," I said.

She kissed my forehead and replied, "You just keep getting prettier every time I see you." After taking my luggage to my room, I collapsed on the bed. As I closed my eyes, my phone lit up with a text from Alex. *"The ocean brings out the best in you. You look radiant, Hannah. Take care of yourself. xxx."* That boy had no idea the effect he had on me. I dozed off into a peaceful sleep for almost three hours. When I woke up, it was almost dark outside. I looked out the window at the sea. The sun was setting, and the sea sparkled with golden specks of the sun. Nothing could compare to that beauty.

"Finally! You're awake!" exclaimed Bev as she stood in front of me, dressed to the nines. I groaned and rubbed my eyes, knowing that she was going to drag me out of the house for some social event. "Aw! No need for that face my friend. Just get dressed and let's go have some fun," she said with a mischievous glint in her eyes. I got up and opened my suitcase, hoping to find a comfortable outfit. But Bev quickly shot down my hoodie choice, urging me to wear something more presentable. I wanted to protest, but instead I gestured for her to pick out an outfit for me. With a smile, she happily obliged and I resigned myself to a night out with my spirited friend.

"You look good Hannah." She had chosen a stylish pair of bootleg jeans, a classic white top, a sleek black leather jacket, and my trusty black sneakers for me to wear.

I thanked her and tied my hair in a high ponytail and said: "I'm ready. Let's go."

There was a red Mercedes parked in front of the house and Levi was standing next to it. Bev glanced at me and smiled. "If I had told you, you wouldn't have come." It was true. I couldn't really blame her for not telling me that we were going out with him beforehand.

"Hi Levi. Nice to see you again." I said, trying to sound polite.

Bev ran into his arms and kissed him on the cheek. "Hi sexy. Did you miss me?" Levi was well mannered and not bad looking, just not my cup of tea. He had a bit of an ego, though not to the extent of being obnoxious.

"Good evening ladies. Get in and let the fun begin." We drove for about ten minutes before he pulled into the driveway of a stunning mansion. I was curious about who the house belonged to, but didn't want to ask. I could hear music playing and people chatting from inside the house. "Are we going to a party?"

"Yes. Come along." Bev sounded nervous. She grasped my hand and led me inside. The house was packed with people, but even so, I could still spot the beauty of the house. As usual, Bev disappeared into the crowd to mingle and I went outside to appreciate the view of the ocean. My phone rang and I was ecstatic to see that it was Alex calling me. "Hi there" I didn't even try to hide the excitement in my voice.

"Hi Hannah. How are you?"

I wanted to tell him that I missed him and that I wished that he was there with me, but instead I said: "I'm good. Having so much fun. I'm actually at a party now." He was silent for a while.

"That's great! Just please be safe and if you plan on drinking, please don't over do it. I'm about to get on a plane, so I'll talk to you later. Let me know when your home safe okay?" I loved the way he cared about me.

"Don't worry. I'll be fine. Have a good flight. Adiós." He laughed.

"Adiós mi amor." He hung up and I was left wondering what *mi amor* meant. Of course I went straight to Google, but before I could type anything, I heard the voice that I really didn't want to hear.

"How is it possible that you got even more beautiful?" I looked up and there he was. In a blue hoodie, which made his eyes even more prominent. I began to walk away, but he caught my hand and pulled me close to him. So close that my heart started racing. Why oh why did this boy still had that effect on me. I tried to walk away again, but then, he kissed me. I pushed him away and without even thinking, I slapped him. "Whoa!" I was just as shocked as he was.

"OMG I'm so sorry!" I said anxiously. He held up his hand.

"No. Don't apologize. I deserved that, but I'd really like a chance to explain Hannah." My mom taught me that everyone deserved a second chance.

"Give me time to think about it." And with those words, I walked away. I couldn't find Bev, so I texted her that I was going home. When I got no response from her after five minutes, I decided to walk home.

I was half way home when I noticed a car following me. Panicked, I began to run. "Hannah, stop! It's just me!" It was Elijah. Irritated, I halted and faced him.

"Why were you following me?" My heart was pounding hard and fast.

"I saw you leaving the party and I knew you wouldn't let me drive you home. I just wanted to make sure you got home safely." Elijah seemed sincerely apologetic, and I felt guilty for my harsh reaction.

ext level or you think he is the special one and want to make your first time together just as special." His words caught me off guard. It felt like I was just kicked in my stomach. I didn't know what to say or how to feel.

"So, how's Spain? And your friend?" I knew that trying to change the subject wasn't the smartest thing to do, but I couldn't think of any other solution.

"Spain is great, and Camila is also great. Hannah, please talk to me. I care about you and I don't want you to get hurt again. Remember, you are my best friend." For some reason, his kind and sweet words annoyed me.

"Thanks, Alex. I have to go though. Talk again soon." For some reason, I felt annoyed at him. I wondered about Camila and what her relationship with Alex entailed.

Chapter 5

"Hey babe, I'm really sorry for leaving you hanging. I ran into this really cute guy, and things got pretty intense," Bev confessed, eyeing me as I sat on the floor. "What's going on, Hannah?" I poured my heart out to her, recounting everything from the party escapade to my conversation with Alex.

She pulled me up and embraced me. "Hang on, I'll be right back." Bev returned with her bag and two glasses.

"What's in the bag?" I asked suspiciously. She smiled mischievously and pulled out a bottle whiskey. "Well, screw it. Pour away," I found myself blurting out, astonished by my own words.

Bev poured the whiskey into the glasses and raised hers in a toast. "Oh, screw it!" We both erupted in laughter.

"Love, I'll be honest with you." Bev said seriously. "This is the way I see it: you are jealous of Camila. You want Alex all to yourself, but you also want Elijah. You desire all the different feelings they both make you feel. You want the romance and the passion, the fireworks and the comfort, the friendship and the love, but, Hannah, the hard truth and reality is that you can't have it all. You can't have your cake and eat it too." I looked at Bev. I was shocked to my core. Partly because what she said was spot on and partly because I never thought she was so insightful and deep. I took my glass and emptied it with one big gulp.

"Keep them coming." I said, handing her the empty glass.

"Rise and shine! It's beautiful out and we have a big day. Get up and get dressed!" Bev announced cheerfully. My head was pounding and my vision blurry.

"I'm not getting out of bed today even if you paid me." I covered my head with the blanket and closed my eyes again.

"Alex is on his way here already. You have to get up and pull yourself together." It was like someone threw a bucket of ice in my face.

"WHAT?!" I screamed, jolting out of bed. "Why is he coming here? I don't understand."

Bev looked at me confused. "You called him last night and asked, no, actually, you begged him to come." I held my head with my hands as it suddenly felt like the room was spinning.

"Oh man. I'm never drinking again." Bev smiled and I could tell she was trying not to laugh.

"Get your pretty little ass in the shower and make it snappy." Bev pinched my cheek playf1ully before she left the room. I couldn't remember calling Alex. The whole night was a blur.

After a much needed shower, I put on my black wide leg pants and white top, quickly tied my hair in a messy bun and went looking for Bev. "Where's Aunt Lillian?" I asked downing a glass icy cold water.

Bev looked at my outfit and rolled her eyes. "She's out for the day and we need to fix your outfit." I couldn't care less about my appearance. I had to figure out what I was going to do. Having both Alex and Elijah near me at the same time was a recipe for disaster.

"Bev, please. I'm stressed out enough." She got up from the sofa and slowly moved toward the door.

"About that whole Alex thing... I was just kidding. You didn't want to get up and I really want to have some fun with my bestie this week." She said while suppressing laughter.

I wanted to punch her right in the face, but I was just too relieved. "Oh thank God!"

I was drinking some strong, black coffee when I received a text from Alex. When I saw his name pop up on my phone, I instantly smiled. *"Hey Beautiful. I miss you so much. Can't wait to see you again. Enjoy the last few days xxx."* I honestly also couldn't wait to see him again, but at the same time I didn't want to leave and be away from Elijah. "Bev, I need you to tell me what to do. I'm going crazy here!"

She came into the kitchen and sat beside me. "Let me guess, you are worried about Elijah coming to our school next year."

It felt like I was going to faint. "Oh no! I forgot about that!" I yelled so loud, the neighbors probably heard me.

"Okay. Firstly, calm down. I know what we have to do. We need to make a list. Pro's and Con's." I thought about it for a while and then I had a vivid lightbulb moment.

"Bev, Alex and I said from the very beginning we would be friends with benefits, but always friends first. We both value our friendship too much to risk it."

Bev lifted both her hands. "So there you have it."

I felt so defeated. "Then why do I feel like someone I loved, just died?" I got up and changed into something Bev would approve of. I chose go with my yellow top, black tights and brown boots. I let my hair hung loose and put on some lip gloss. I chose red.

"So freaking hot!" Bev said, applauding.

I smiled warmly at her. "Thanks, Bev. Let's go for drinks and then go dancing. I need to get my mind of this mess I've gotten myself into."

Bev's eyes lit up and she grabbed her bag. "I love you!" She pulled me by my hand and we practically ran out the house. She locked up and then took out her phone. "I'm just ordering us an cab. I don't feel like walking today." I nodded and turned toward the ocean.

I closed my eyes and once again, took it all in. "Oh I really love this. Nothing will ever compare."

Bev smiled wickedly. "Not even hot and steamy sex with Alex?" That was the last thing I expected her to say.

"OMG it's like Sophie's Choice." We both burst out laughing and it felt good. Just like old times. Before everything got so complicated. Before passion and butterflies, lust and love and before fireworks and boys.

"Come on, you have to answer." She had that determined look in her eyes. I thought about it for a while.

"Okay. I want sex with Alex on the beach." I don't think I've ever seen Bev laugh that hard before. She was out of breath when she finally stopped.

"Wow Hannah. It must be real good then, hey?"

I looked at the ocean again. "It's great. Really freakin' great."

It was around 12pm when we parked in front of the mall. "Lets first go shopping." Bev paid the cab driver and we got out of the car. "How many clothes can one person have? Seriously. Your closet probably can't even close properly at this point."

Bev laughed and took my hand. "No, my dear friend, we are going shopping for some much needed lingerie for you." I got excited thinking about how Alex would react to me in my new and sexy lingerie. Then I realized that we'd probably have to stop the benefits side of our friendship.

"Oh what's the point? I won't be needing them anytime soon." If I chose to be with Elijah, I couldn't continue being friends with benefits with Alex anymore. It wouldn't be right.

"So, you and Alex won't be doing it anymore? And what about Elijah? Isn't he worthy?" I knew she was joking, but I really felt confused.

"I don't think I fully trust him yet. But we never know what the future holds. So, let's go shopping." Almost two hours later, we walked out of the store. We got lingerie, slippers, pj's and some cartoon themed socks. Bev carefully selected everything, well except the socks.

We went to a Starbucks nearby and ordered some coffee. "This aroma reminds me of Alex. Did I tell you...." Bev held her hand in the air.

"No more talk about Alex. You need to detox." She was right. I knew she was, but it was difficult. I didn't want to cut him off completely. He deserved more than that. I took out my phone and texted him: "*Hi there. I miss you too. We have so much to talk about. Enjoy the rest of your week. Adiós.*"

"Let's walk to the pub. I need some fresh air." I suggested hopefully, but Bev shook her head. I could see she wouldn't change her mind, so I just enjoyed the rest of my coffee in silence.

"I'll order us another Uber. Just sit tight."

I was relieved to see that the pub was almost empty when we arrived. Bev asked the bartender for two Long Island Ice teas. She always got her way with male bartenders. They couldn't resist her, so he didn't even asked for our ID's. "Cheers to us beautiful babes, living our best lives!" I lifted my glass "To us!" Bev walked over to the Alexa speaker at the end of the counter.

"Alexa, play 'Crowded Room' by Megan Trainer." I got up and joined Bev dancing. It was basically the only song we both liked. She was into pop music and I liked R&B. Several drinks later, Elijah and Don walked in. By then, we were already tipsy and having a blast. I jumped into Elijah's arms and wrapped my legs around him.

"You are so damn hot!" I kissed him like I always kissed Alex, like my life depended on it. Bev pulled on my arm.

"Lets do shots!" I threw my arms in the air.

"Hell yeah!" I'm not sure how many tequila shots we drank that night. All I knew was that I was having fun, drinking and dancing with my bestie and the boy I liked. Later that night when Elijah dropped me off at home, we made out and things got really heated. He went to second base again and this time, I allowed him to. He then went to third. The windows of the car was covered with vapor. I climbed on top of him and he started kissing my neck . He unhooked my bra underneath my top.

"Want to go to my house? I'm home alone." He whispered breathlessly. I really wanted him, but for some reason, I hesitated.

"If you're not ready, I'll understand. Please don't feel obligated." He sounded disappointed, but sincere. I kissed him again.

"Yes, I want to. Let me just first text Bev." I climbed of him and texted Bev telling her where I'll be.

His house was huge. It also had a gorgeous view of the ocean. He unlocked the door and turned the lights on. He then lifted me in his arms and carried me upstairs. His room was a typical boy's room. There was posters of cars on the walls, trophies on his dressing table and clothes in a bundle on the floor in the back corner. He gently laid me on his bed and locked his bedroom door. I started undressing, but he stopped me by taking my hands. "Allow me." His voice was hoarse, which made me want him even more. He climbed on top of me and we kissed. He slowly undressed me, while kissing each part of my body he uncovered. We made love and it felt like we were the only two people in the world.

When we came out of the room, I heard music coming from downstairs. "What's happening?" Elijah closed his bedroom door behind him.

"The guys wanted to hang out. Bev's probably down there too." I was overwhelmed with anger, I almost slapped him again.

"So you knew they were coming over and you still made love to me in your room? Everyone will know what we did once we walk down those stairs. This was a huge mistake." I turned to walk away, but he pulled me back and kissed me.

"I'm sorry Hannah. I just really wanted to be with you. I... I think I'm I love with you." And just like that, I was under his spell again. That boy had a way of hurting me and then effortlessly pulling me back in. Was it his mesmerizing eyes? Or maybe it was the way he carried himself. Whatever is was, it had a powerful hold on me.

It was my second last day in Massachusetts. I was on the beach, sitting in the sand and enjoying the magical view. I was so deep in thought that I didn't hear Bev walking up behind me. "Are you bummed that its almost time to go home?" I honestly didn't know the answer to that question.

"Well, I will miss this. I always do. The beach is my happy place , you know. When I'm here, I forget about everything else. It's just me and the ocean."

Bev cleared her throat and then looked at me with a serious expression on her face. "Hannah, I know Elijah is sweet, romantic and very hot, but he also hurt you very badly in the past. Just please be cautious." I didn't want get into it at that moment, so I just nodded and gave her a hug.

"Just sit with me and let's enjoy this gorgeous view for a moment." I haven't heard from Elijah since the night before and I felt a little uneasy about it, so I decided to tell Bev what happened and how I was feeling.

"OMG! Oh honey, I really wish you told me this earlier!" She covered her face with her hands and I got really worried. "Last night, before I came home, I saw Elijah and Don talking. He told Don something, they laughed and then they high fived. I walked closer to ask them what was going on, but Elijah saw me and bolted. I didn't think anything of it at the time, but now...."

I knew exactly what happened. There was no doubt in my mind and I was so furious. I immediately took out my phone and texted him: *"You are such a pig. I hate you. Getting into my pants was the ultimate goal huh? Well, congrats jerk, you succeeded. Never contact me again."*

"I can't believe I was so stupid. I really thought he cared, even loved me." I couldn't hold back the tears. Bev hugged me tight and I just completely broke down.

Chapter 6

The next morning, I woke up early. I made myself some coffee, got dressed and went outside to watch the sunrise. Just then, phone rang. It was Alex, video calling me. "Hannah, what's wrong? You're eyes are swollen. Have you been crying?" Seeing him and hearing his voice, made me cry all over again. I tried to stop, but I couldn't. I tried to speak, but I couldn't. "Okay, I just landed in Boston. Should I come get you?" It just amazed me – the special bond we shared. He cared so much.

I forced myself to stop crying. "No, it's fine. We are taking the bus back to Boston tomorrow morning." I could see the worry in his eyes.

"Please Hannah. Just allow me to come get you." He pleaded.

I looked at the sunrise again. "Well, enjoying the sunset on the beach with you wouldn't be the worst thing in the world. Thanks Alex. I can always count on you." After we hung up, I went back inside and took a shower. I put on a pair of skinny jeans, a pink hoodie with Tinkerbelle on the front and my pink pumps. I received a text from Elijah: *"Can we please talk? Can I come over?"*

I decided not to reply. Bev and Aunt Lillian were still asleep, so I made breakfast for us. I fried some eggs and bacon. It was Bev's favorite. I was deep in thought when I heard a car pull up in front of the house. It was Elijah. At first, I didn't want to go outside, but then I decided to face him, get closure and finally move on. He saw me and got out of the car.

"Good morning, Hannah. Thank you for seeing me." I avoided looking into his eyes. It had the ability to make me oblivious to the heartache he was capable of causing.

"You didn't give me much of a choice. Now please just say your say and go. I have to start packing."

He put his hands on my arms, but I backed away. "Hannah, I'm so sorry. I don't have any excuse. I have this habit of screwing up good things in my life for no reason, but I'm trying to be a better person."

I gathered all my strength, looked him in the eyes and emphasized each word as it left my mouth. "You sure broke us. This thing between us, is over." I turned around and walked away. My feet felt heavy, almost like it knew I was walking away from my first great love. It was hard as hell, but the love I had for him, wasn't good for my heart and at some point, we have to cut our losses and move on.

When I entered the kitchen Bev was making coffee and Aunt Lillian was buttering some toast. "Good morning Hannah. Did you sleep well?" Aunt Lillian's voice was like medicine for my wounded heart.

"Good morning ladies." I tied so sound happy. "Bev, I have some exciting news. Alex is coming to pick us up later today. I think he might be driving here already." She looked relieved. Taking the bus was one of the things she really dreaded. "Oh thank God! We'd better start packing after breakfast then." I nodded and took a sip of my coffee.

"There's no need to hurry, I want to take him on a tour of the town and show him the sunset on the beach before we leave." Bev smirked and I knew exactly what she was thinking about. The whole sex with Alex on the beach thing I said the other day. I playfully hit her on the arm.

"I don't even want to know." Aunt Lillian said while she shook her head and we all started laughing.

"Well, I have a few things I want to do before we leave, so I'll quickly pack my stuff and then head out. Is that okay?" Bev asked.

Aunt Lillian nodded. "No problem Honey. Have a great last day."

I finished packing and was about to call Alex, when my phone rang. It was Elijah. "What is it Elijah?" I didn't even try to hide the annoyance in my voice.

"Can I please come over? I really don't want to leave things between us like this." I didn't want to see him again. I was ready to move on.

"No Elijah. Let's just move on." I heard him sigh on the other end. "Hannah, I am in love with you and I won't stop trying to win back your heart. Just know that. I'll see you when school starts." I hung up. It was going to be hard to see him everyday and not be with him. Even now, when I'm so furious at him, I still missed him.

"Hannah! I'm going out for a while. Please lock the door behind me!" Aunt Lillian was out the door before I could say anything. I went to lock the door, but just then, Alex' car pulled up. I squealed and ran out the door and straight into his arms.

He lifted me into the air. "*Me amor, te ves tan hermosa.*" He put me down and perused me from head to toe.

"I can't tell you how happy I am to see you! Come inside." He locked the car and we walked into the house.

"Something to drink?" I walked into the kitchen and poured myself some water.

"No thanks. I'm good." I noticed that he had a tan. He looked extra handsome that way.

"So, what does that mean? What you said earlier in spanish." I asked in anticipation.

He smiled and looked around the kitchen. "Some juice would be nice if you have some." I checked in the fridge and poured him some orange juice. "My love, you look beautiful. That's what it means." I spilled some juice on the counter and he laughed.

"Thank you Alex." I felt so shy and I hated it. He could probably tell because he changed the subject.

"So what's the plans for the day?" he asked when I handed him the juice and smiled sweetly.

"Well, my dear friend, I'm taking you on a tour through beautiful Massachusetts. And for the grand finale, I'm taking you to my happy place to show you something that will change your life."

He seemed genuinely excited. "I can't wait. Let me just go to the bathroom first then we can leave." I showed him the way and then popped into my room to check my hair and put on some lip gloss. He came up behind me quietly. "So, this is your room? I like it. It's nice and cozy."

I looked at him and then at the bed. I contemplated pushing him onto it and jumping on top of him. It took all my strength to refrain from doing what I wanted to.

"Yes, I love it. Come on, let's go." I walked out as quick as I could.

He pulled me close to him and whispered in my ear: "I saw the way you looked at me and then the bed. I know what you wanted to do." He smiled wickedly and opened the car door for me.

"Well, at least I was able to control myself, unlike some people I know." He laughed loudly and then we were off. I took him everywhere I could think of. Except the places we might run into Elijah.

I felt my stomach rumbling and suggested we get something to eat. We found a nice little pizza place nearby and went inside. "So, Hannah, tell me what's happening with you and Elijah." He was looking through the menu when he asked me that loaded question.

"He is a riddle that I cant seem to figure out. One moment he's this sweet and romantic guy, then suddenly he turns into a jerk"

Alex laughed. "All men are like that, Hannah." The waiter came and took our order. I got a chocolate milkshake and small pepperoni pizza. Alex took a Coke and a large pepperoni pizza.

"With us it's like two steps forward and three steps back. I think in some masochistic way, I actually like the thrill of the unknown. Until it hurts me, that is."

Alex had a serious expression on his face. "Sounds toxic Hannah. Is he worth it? Does he make you feel all the feels?"

I thought about it for a while and then I smiled. "I get butterflies in my stomach each time we kiss. My hearts goes wild in my chest when he touches me and he said that he's in love with me."

Alex took my hands in his and smiled. "It doesn't matter what you decide. I'll always be here for you. Just please, put yourself first. Do what makes you happy." I was even more confused after our conversation, but decided to not think about it any further.

After our meal, we drove down to the beach. I took off my sandals and ran toward the water. "Come on!" I called out at Alex. He came running behind me, picked me up and twirled around playfully. We sat on the sand, side by side. "This beauty will forever change your life."

He smiled and put his arm around my shoulders. "Thanks for sharing your happy place with me, Hannah." We spent the next few moments in silence, just looking at the blending of sea and sky. "We should get going. We still have a long drive ahead of us." He said, as he got up.

Back at the house, Bev and Aunt Lillian were in the kitchen, talking. When she saw Alex, she squealed and gave him a hug. "Thanks so much for rescuing me from a dreadful bus ride. I owe you one. Come, meet my grandma." While they were chatting, I went to my room to get my luggage and I got this sudden urge to call Elijah. I wished that I could just get him out of my system. Why did I have to love him this much. I pulled out my phone and texted him. "*I'm leaving now. So, just wanted you to know that I forgive you. Please try to be a better person in the future. I believe in you.*"

Chapter 7

Bev was sleeping on the backseat almost the whole drive. Alex was telling me about Spain, how beautiful it was there and how I should go with him next time. "I would love that. Thanks Alex." I opened a packet of marshmallows Alex bought earlier. "Are you excited about being a senior? I sure am. Just one more year of Albert High." I was excited, but also sad. I'll miss high school and being close to my mom, Bev and Alex.

"Yeah, but I'm scared of the unknown, you know?" I confessed.

Alex was the adventurous kind. He was like a more subtle, male version of Bev. College would be easy for them. Probably for Elijah too. He was confident and charming. The girls would go crazy over him, I'm sure. Even at school too. I'll have to brace myself. Just thinking about him with another girl made my heart ache. Maybe I should give him another chance. Maybe I can help him become better. "Penny for your thoughts?" Alex's voice pulled me back to the present.

"I was just thinking about College life and whether I'd fit in." He pinched my cheek playfully.

"You won't fit in Hannah, you were made to stand out!" Its when he said things like that, that made me want to kiss the hell out of him.

"You always know just how to cheer me up, don't you? I really appreciate you Alex."

When we arrived in Boston, I woke Bev. "Rise and shine my friend. We're home."

She sat up and yawned. "That was quick. Please drop me off first Alex. I have to go to the loo." She winked at me. And I knew exactly what she was thinking. I just smiled and shrugged at her. Alex dropped me off next.

"So, can I expect you tonight? My parents are only coming back on Sunday." I was still so confused about where things stood with Elijah, but I really missed Alex and wanted to spend time with him before school start again.

"Yes. I'll just catch up with my mom and take a shower. I'll text you when I'm ready." He helped my carry my luggage inside and then he kissed me on the cheek.

"See you later." It only took a kiss on the cheek from this boy to leave my knees weak. How can I have this much chemistry with him, when I'm so deeply in love with Elijah?

"Baby? You're back!" I ran into my mom's arms and hugged her tightly

"I missed you mom!" She took my hand and led met into the kitchen. On the table were cottage pie and tiramisu for dessert. "Mom! You made my favorites!" She smiled and walked toward the oven. When she opened it, the smell of blueberry muffins escaped and I squealed. "You are the best mom ever!" I grabbed a plate and bowl. I dished some cottage pie in the plate and tiramisu in the bowl.

"So, how was Massachusetts? And Lillian?" I swallowed my food and took a sip of juice.

"Aunt Lillian is great. Massachusetts was interesting, but the ocean is very well. It sends regards." She laughed and touched my cheek lovingly.

"I missed you so much my baby. Now eat up. She looked at her watch and got up. "Honey, I have to go to the hospital, there's an urgent case. Do you mind?" I shook my head. This actually works out good. Now I don't have feel guilty about going to Alex's.

"No worries mom. I'm going to Alex's anyway." She nodded and gathered all her files and handbag on the counter.

"Have a good night baby." I finished my pie and dished some tiramisu and muffins into take away boxes for me and Alex. My luggage were still standing in the passage and I really didn't want unpack. I carried it to my room and jumped into the shower. I took my Mickey mouse t shirt and black shorts out my closet. Luckily Bev wasn't there to comment on my outfit. I put on my white sneakers and left my hair loose. My phone rang just as I was about to text Alex.

It was him calling. "Hi. I'm ready." I tried to disguise the excitement in my voice.

"I'll be right there." I put on some lip gloss, grabbed the take away boxes and went to wait for him outside. I had just locked the door when he pulled up. He rolled down the window. " My queen. Your chariot awaits!" I laughed as I walked to his car. As per usual, he got out and opened the passenger door for me.

"What's in the boxes? I'm starving!"

I handed him the boxes. "See for yourself." He immediately opened the boxes.

"Oh man! This looks delicious. Thanks Hannah." He switched on the car and drove off. As we entered the house, I heard a movie was playing om the television. "Make yourself at home. And by that I mean take of all your clothes." I inhaled sharply and he started laughing. "Hannah! I'm only joking!" I rolled my eyes, took the remote and sat on the carpet.

"As punishment, you'll watch a sappy romcom with me." He quickly grabbed the remote control from my hand and smirked.

"I actually already have a movie in mind." I opened the take away box and took a big bite of a muffin. I almost chocked when I saw the title of the movie appear on the screen. "*Fifty shades of Grey.*" He looked at me amused.

"Yeah, yeah, very funny Alex. Please put on a real movie." He looked at me confused and then sat next to me.

"Hannah, this is a real movie. In fact, it's as real as it gets." He handed me a cushion, trying to suppress a smile. I grabbed it from his hand and put it under my head as I laid down. He took the other box with the dessert.

"Please save some for me too." I said. Tiramisu was his favorite dessert too. Well, that and mudpie. He heaped some on a spoon and fed me.

"Now you're done. No more dessert for you tonight, except...." He leaned down and kissed me. Slowly and passionately. A tingling sensation took over my body. I wanted to get up and on top of him, but he held me down and I stroked his biceps.

"I have to have you now." My voice was shaking. I hardy recognized it.

"Patience me amór." He kissed my neck, pushed up my shirt and kissed my chest. He then moved down to my stomach. He kept moving downwards. It was so intense, I had to shut my mouth with my hands to keep from screaming. I couldn't take it anymore. Gathering all my strength, I pushed him off me, quickly got undressed and climbed on top of him. It was incredible. Each time with him was different, but in a good way. No, in a great way.

As we laid there, naked, side by side, Camila popped into my head. "Alex, can I ask you something?" He turned his head and looked at me.

"Of course you can. Always." I wasn't sure that it was the right time to ask him about her, but I really wanted to know.

"So, did you hook up with Camila while you were in Spain?" I felt so stupid saying the words out loud. What difference did it make anyway. Bev was right. I wanted my cake and eat it too.

"I mean, we did hook up once or twice." I tried to act like I didn't care, but I wasn't that good an actress.

"Do you have a picture of her?" He reached for his phone and showed me a picture. She was wearing a black bikini. Her long brown hair was hanging loose and she had blue eyes. Her skin was tanned a beautiful light brown. "Wow Alex! She's model-perfect!" He looked at the picture and then turned to me.

"She doesn't have anything on you though." I blushed hard. I really wished he'd stop looking at me. It was like he was enjoying seeing me embarrassed, so I kissed him for distraction, but as usual, the magnetic pull took over and we were at it again.

It was already passed midnight when I checked my phone. "Wow, it's late. Can you please drop me of at home?" He nodded while putting on this clothes. I admired his body for a few seconds before I got dressed too.

"Tonight was great Hannah. Thanks for the dessert...and the dessert." He winked at me and smiled wickedly. And the blushing began again. I didn't want him to have this kind of effect on me anymore. I wanted to try again with Elijah.

"Alex, I was thinking of giving it another go with Elijah. Are you cool with that?" He didn't look at me when he answered.

"Yeah, I mean it's your choice. You know I support you." He sounded genuinely sincere.

"Okay, so you know that means we have to stop the benefit side of our friendship, right?"

He froze and then looked at me with an expression I couldn't quite figure out. "Well, I guess it was bound to happen sometime right? It won't be easy, but for you, I'll make the sacrifice." I smiled and walked toward the front door. The atmosphere was so heavy and I felt like I just lost a limb, like my body was incomplete. But what was I supposed to do? I couldn't have it both ways. It wouldn't be right. I just hoped that we would be able to keep the special bond we had, our close friendship.

When I entered my house, my mom was in the kitchen, making coffee. "Hannah, my baby, come sit please. I have to tell you something." I knew right away that it wasn't good news. If it were, she'd start with "I have some great news" or "you'll never guess..." I sat down at the table and waited for her to start talking. "Baby, I really didn't want to tell you this, but I have no choice. Your... Dave... is sick, really sick. He is in hospital." Dave was my father. He left me and my mom when I was two years old. I didn't call him dad. To me he wasn't worthy of the title.

"Mom, I really don't understand why you are telling me this. I barely know the man." I could tell she was very nervous by the way she was fidgeting with her fingers.

"Well, he wants to see you. I know you don't owe him anything, but I think you should go. Fix things with him before it's too late." I couldn't believe that my mom expected that from me.

The man had an affair with one of her close friends and when they got caught, he decided to leave us. He married the other woman and they started a new family. In all these years, he never reached out - no phone calls, no birthday cards, no contact. Absolutely nothing, but now that he is sick, I should drop everything and run to be at his side. "Mom, there's no way in hell I'm going to see that man. I'm sorry. I don't have a dad and I've made peace with that a long time ago." I could see that she wanted to talk more, but she just stared down at the table silently.

She was such a compassionate person. It drove me crazy sometimes. She forgave Dave almost immediately after his deceit. "Ultimately it's your decision. I just don't want you to regret anything later. So, please, just take time and think about it. For now, let's go to bed. I'm sure you're exhausted. I love you baby." I gave her a long hug and then went to my room.

My lit up and revealed a text from Elijah. *"I can't stop thinking about you. I miss you."* I couldn't stop myself from smiling. Oh what I wouldn't give to be in that boy's arms. He had a way of making me feel safe and content. I decided to text him back. *"I miss you too. And I really wish you were here. Take care."* I felt overly tired, but I wanted to take a bath and clear my head. That night I dreamt about Elijah. We were walking on the beach, holding hands. No one spoke, we just walked in complete silence. I felt at peace, happy and light. We were both completely dressed in white. The sun was setting, the water was sparkling and the sea breeze was gentle on my skin. In that moment, everything was perfect and then... I woke up.

I was busy unpacking when my phone rang. It was an unfamiliar number. I hesitated before answering. "Hello, Hannah?" The male voice on the other side sounded vaguely familiar. "It's me, dad" I froze. For a moment I was totally speechless.

"I... I don't have a dad. What can I do for you Dave?" I could hear him sigh on the other end.

"Could you please come see me? I'm really sick and I need to talk to you." Again, I couldn't find any words to say. "Please think about it Hannah."

He sounded so desperate. Did he really want to make amends so badly? Could it be possible that he desired my forgiveness so desperately? I just hung up and continued unpacking, but his words kept echoing in my mind over and over. The man I knew was a selfish person. He only cared about his other family. Never, not even once did he reach out to me or my mom. What was even the point of seeing him now? What difference would it make? I really didn't feel anything towards him. Not anger. Not hate. Not love. Nothing. Something about the whole scenario didn't make sense to me. I was still deep in thought, when Bev burst into my room. "Good morning, sunshine!" She gave me a hug and then laid down on my bed.

"Okay baby, what's wrong?" There was no point in lying to her, so I told her the whole story. Bev was the only one in my life who knew about Dave besides my family. She was just sitting there in silence . I could tell that she didn't know what to say. "I'm so sorry Hannah. Whatever you decide to do, you know I'll be here for you." Bev may be a little shallow and childish at times, but when I needed her, she was always there. She never judged or betrayed me and that meant the world.

"Thank you Bev. You are so amazing. I put the last of my clothes into my closet and sat next to Bev on the bed. "I dreamt about Elijah last night. I miss him." She suddenly jumped up from the bed, super excited.

"You don't need to miss him! School starts in a few days! In the meantime, you can text and video call him. How about we get make overs for senior year?" The idea of a make over excited me. "Maybe a new haircut…" I was interrupted by my phone ringing. It was Elijah.

"Good morning." I couldn't hide the excitement in my voice.

"Good morning, Hannah. I just wanted to hear your voice. You good?" I told him about Dave. I was expecting a similar response from him as I got from Bev, but he completely surprised me with his response. "Hannah, he stays your father. When we met I told you I speak my mind. So that's why I'm telling you that you'll regret it deeply if you don't go." I wanted to yell at him for telling me what to do, but on the other side, I respected the fact that he was honest and spoke frankly.

Chapter 8

When I hung up the phone, Bev was asleep on my bed. My mind was in a clutter, and I desperately wanted to sit by the ocean and just be for a while. I needed to make a decision about Dave. He was in Portland, where he married that woman and they started their own family. Portland was two hours away. I would have to take the bus or train if I decided to go see him. I refused to inconvenience my mother for the sake of the man who broke her heart and left her to raise their baby on her own. What on earth could he say to make that okay?

School started in four days and if I decided to go see him, it would have to be before then. I laid next to Bev and texted Alex. Maybe he could help me decide. He was so mature and insightful. It wasn't long before he replied. "*Hi Hannah. All I can say is that even though I don't have a close relationship with my dad, I'm glad I have him in my life. And I think that you should give Dave a chance. You might be glad you did.*" It wasn't exactly what I wanted to hear, but I guess he was right. I mean, it wasn't like I had anything to lose. I would go and listen to what he had to say. Then I'll come back home and everything would be back to normal.

"Bev... wake up." I tried to woke her gently, but she was sleeping so deeply that I decided to leave her be. I heard mom in the kitchen. She was baking rusks. "Good morning mom. I'm so glad you slept in. Even superheroes need to rest." She burst out laughing.

"Good morning, Sweetheart. How are you today?" I poured myself some coffee end sat down at the table. "Mom, I've decided to go see Dave. I want to go tomorrow already. Just get it over with, you know?" I knew it sounded harsh, but it wasn't my intention. It was just the way I felt.

"Okay, Honey. I understand. We can leave tomorrow morning. And don't even try to argue with me. I'm not letting you take a train or bus to Portland." I felt nervous. There was no way for me to prepare for what was about to come. It wasn't like an exam I could study for. I just hoped that it wouldn't be long. That he would just say his piece so I could return to my life and move forward. I really wanted to start senior year drama-free. Hopefully, his wife and kids wouldn't be there. Seeing him was one thing, but making small talk with his new family was something I definitely didn't want to do. According to mom, he had two sons. I didn't even know their names. I didn't want or need any siblings. I loved being an only child.

"Hon, we still need to talk about college too. Just let me know when you're ready." I didn't know if I'd ever be ready to leave home, but I nodded.

"Mom, I'm going for a walk. Please tell Bev that I tried to wake her and that I'm going to see Dave tomorrow." I grabbed my phone and headed out the door. I didn't have a particular destination in mind.

As I walked past a park, I thought about Elijah, and I realized that I would see him in four days. The thought of being in his arms again was thrilling. I wondered how the other girls would react when they saw that gorgeous boy with nerdy old me. At least I had something to look forward to.

I'd been walking for almost twenty minutes when I received a text from Bev. "*I'm so sorry for falling asleep, babe. How about I stick you for a milkshake to make up for it?*" I just wanted to be alone with my thoughts for a while, so I replied: "*Hi Bev. No worries. I just need to be alone for a while. Raincheck on that milkshake. Love.*"

There were so many things I needed to do that year. I had to apply to colleges, make a final decision about a career path, and get my driver's license, but seeing Dave was not one of them. However, I decided to go and see him. Not for him, but for my mom. I could see that she wanted me to go and, although I didn't agree with her, I respected her. I wanted to go as soon as possible to get the whole thing over and done with so everything could return to normal. I decided to go the next day.

When I got back home, it was already noon. After I told Mom what I decided, I went to my room and watched a movie to get my mind off everything.

The next morning, I woke up very early. I made myself some coffee and breakfast. My mom was in the shower already. She was almost never late for anything. She really amazed me. Her ex husband betrayed her with her best friend and then, instead of asking for a second chance, he just walked right out of their marriage and our family, yet here she was, encouraging me to go see him. My mom was my everything. I didn't even needed or wanted a father. She was just everything. I remember when I was still in middle school, there was a father and daughter dance. That was the first time I really resented Dave, but my mom stepped up and accompanied me to the dance. I thought it would be weird and the other kids would make fun of me, but she was super cool and I realized that she'd be all I'd ever need.

After showering, I put on a pair of jeans and my red Micky Mouse t shirt. I tied my hair in a high ponytail and put my white sandals on. My mom knocked on my bedroom door. "Morning, Baby. Are you almost done? We have to get going." I grabbed my phone and headed out the door.

"Good morning, my dearest mother." I hugged her tightly. I didn't let it show, but I was dreading the day ahead. My mom was wearing a blue maxi dress and she looked radiant, she always did. I wondered whether she'd go with me to hear what Dave had to say, not that I expected her to. He really hurt her and if it was me, I would never want to see him again.

In the car, I texted Bev, Alex and Elijah to inform them that I was on my way to see Dave. Bev and Alex replied, but Elijah didn't and I really wanted him to. It felt like my love for him was growing deeper by the day and that scared me. I wanted him to be part of any and everything in my life.

"Honey, are you worried about seeing Dave?" I really wasn't.

"No. I don't feel anything mom. I just want it to be over." I couldn't figure out what he would want to say to me after all these years? That he was sorry? What difference would that make? It would probably make him feel better and I wasn't even sure if he deserved that, but I had to push through. I had no choice. "Mom, I don't want to stay there long okay? When he said his peace, we'll go right?" I knew my mom would agree. She understood how I felt.

"Okay, my baby. No problem. You are already making a huge sacrifice by seeing him." I felt relieved. I would just listen to what he had to say and try to be as polite as possible.

When we pulled up at the hospital, my heart suddenly started racing and I felt nauseous. I always felt this way before a big test. I took some deep breaths to calm down before getting out of the car.

"Don't be nervous, baby. You did a good thing by coming today. You should feel proud of yourself." She always knew just how to make me feel better. I hated hospitals, the smell, the way it was always so cold, and the anxious expressions on people's faces in the waiting areas. Mom knew exactly which room Dave was in. It didn't surprise me. They were communicating a lot before we came. She entered the room and I heard his voice as he greeted her.

"Hi, Addison. You look good." I was standing in the hallway. My legs didn't want to move. I contemplated turning around, but then I heard my mom's voice.

"Hi Dave. I brought someone very special with me." I knew that that was my cue. I had to go in. I had to face the man that abandoned me when I was two years old.

He looked pale and thin, but even through that, I could tell he was a handsome man. He had blue eyes and dark brown hair. He looked at me and started crying. "You are absolutely gorgeous, just like your mom." I felt so uncomfortable.

"Thank you." My voice was very soft and shaky. I sat on one of the chairs beside his bed. "So, I'm here Dave. What do you want to talk about?" My mom shot me a *"what's wrong with you"* look, but I didn't really care. I wanted to get out of there as soon as possible.

"Straight to the point huh? I like that. You actually got that from me." I shrugged and gestured with my hand for him to keep talking. My mom buried her face in her hands. "So, Hannah, the thing is I have been diagnosed with end-stage renal disease. It is a permanent condition of kidney failure." I felt sorry for him. Even he didn't deserve that, but the fact that he waited for something like that to happen before contacting me, wasn't right either. "The reason I asked you to come, is because I need a kidney transplant and I was hoping you'd get tested. Unfortunately my other kids aren't a match and they can't donate." I couldn't believe what I was hearing. What a nerve this man had to ask me for anything, let alone a vital organ. He didn't even apologize or tried to explain his actions from all those years ago. He didn't ask about school or anything about my life for that matter.

Before I knew it, I was overwhelmed with rage and jumped to my feet, yelling at him. "Are you kidding me?! I thought you wanted to apologize and make amends for the hell you put me and my mom through. And you actually have the guts to ask me for something? You can go to hell for all I care!" I stormed out of the room without a second thought and without turning back once, I walked straight to our car. I came. I listened . I was done.

My mom didn't say anything when she returned and unlocked the car. I was expecting her to tell me how wrong I was for disrespecting Dave like that. Instead, she was silent. We got in the car and she drove off. "Please just say something mom. I hate the silent treatment. I know what I did was wrong and I'm s..." She held her hand in the air to stop me.

"No Hannah. He was wrong. He was unbelievably selfish and cruel. I can not believe he would ask you for something so huge without discussing it with me first. I'm so sorry for forcing you to come here today." I could see she wanted to cry and my heart broke for her. She only meant well.

"Mom, please don't cry. I decided to see Dave. It's not your fault he is such a butt hole" She burst out laughing and I felt at ease again. Seeing her smile and laugh, made me happy too.

Chapter 9

I did some research about renal disease and the procedure of donating a kidney. I didn't even know if I wanted to get tested, but I knew I had to. What kind of person would I be if I didn't help someone, anyone in need? I didn't feel bad about yelling at Dave though. He deserved that. He could've handled the situation much better, nonetheless, I couldn't refuse to get tested. It goes against my values. "Mom, can I get tested at a hospital in Boston or do I have to go back to Portland?"

My mom looked at me shocked . Then she stopped the car at the side of the road. "Honey, please don't feel obligated to do anything. Put yourself first. Remember there are all sorts of risks with operations and not even to mention all the sacrifices you'd have to make." I appreciated the fact that she put me first and cared so much.

"I understand mom. I'll just get tested for now and if I am a match for Dave, we'll go through all the information together, before making a decision, okay?" She nodded warily and turned the car back on.

"Okay then. I just want you to be careful honey."

The rest of the drive back home, we listened to old love songs on the radio. Usually my mom would sing along, but this time, she was quiet. She had an amazing voice and she always said that singing made her feel joy on another level. When she sang, my world was all right. It calmed me just like the ocean did. Her silence made me nervous and I couldn't seem to think of anything appropriate to say. I didn't want to upset her any further, but all I could think about was Dave and the kidney transplant.

Back at home, I called Alex and asked him to come over. I didn't want to go to his house because we'd be alone there and I didn't trust myself to be alone with him just yet. It was a strange feeling knowing that I would see him, but not kiss him or hold him. I wanted too so badly, especially when I felt so defeated. It was actually an opportunity to see whether our friendship could still work without any of the benefits. It was kind of weird that I chose to talk to him instead of Bev and Elijah and I wondered if maybe on some level I actually wanted him to comfort me in a way that only he could, but it couldn't happen. My heart belonged to Elijah, I was sure of it.

"Are you serious Hannah? He really asked you for your kidney? Wow. This guy is unbelievable!" Alex's voice was filled with disbelief.

"I know. It was the last thing I expected, but now I need to get tested to see if I am even a match for Dave before anything else." Alex assured me that he would be with me every step of the way. He even offered to make an appointment at the hospital and drive me there.

We were sitting on my bed and I could feel the tension building up between us with every passing minute. I tried to avoid eye contact with him, but he lifted me chin with his finger and looked me in my eyes. "I know you feel it too Hannah. All you have to do is ask." I could feel the burning sensation in my stomach and all I wanted to do was grab him and kiss him, but I controlled myself and got up.

"I'm really tired. This day was exhausting. Would you mind if I take a bath quickly? You can watch a movie in the meantime. I don't want you to go just yet." Even though it was difficult to be in his presence without physically being with him, he made me feel so much better. I needed him with me.

I laid in the bath tub with my eyes closed and imagined what it would be like if Elijah was with me. Would he wash my back while I sat between his legs? Would he softly kiss my neck and run his fingers playfully down my chest? If it was Alex, I knew he would. He would touch me all over until it would feel like I want to explode. He had a way of making me ache for him inside me. The chemistry we had was all consuming and undeniable. Just the mere touch of his hand on my body was enough for me to lose my mind. How the hell did I go from Elijah to Alex in zero seconds? What was happening? My heart longed for Elijah, but my body longed for Alex? I needed to check myself. Someone was bound to get hurt if I continued to think that way.

When I got back in my room, Alex was on his phone. A horror movie was playing and he gestured for me to come lay beside him. I hesitated because I was so afraid I'd lose all control being so close to him, but I obliged. His smell, his touch, the way he held me while he told me the plot of the movie, laying so damn close to him, it was all so difficult. He turned to me and said: "There's something on your face." He then gently wiped some soap from my cheek and that was it, I couldn't contain myself anymore.

Just as I was about to kiss him, his phone lit up. I saw it was a text from Camila. "Oh, I thought you guys only had like a summer fling." I sounded so jealous and I wished I could take back my words. He smirked and I knew he also heard the jealousy in my voice.

"We're just chatting a bit. Nothing serious." He laid back down and his hand touched mine. It was like sparks were flying all over the room. We instantly kissed. It was like we were in the dessert for a long time and finally got some water to drink. It felt so good, so damn good. I wanted more, so much more, but just then I heard my mom calling me.

"I should've just gone over to your house." I said, irritated and he erupted in laughter.

My legs felt heavy as I walked to the kitchen. "Hi mom."

"Hi baby. Are you alone? Thought I heard you speaking to someone." Mom liked Alex a lot. I had a feeling that she knew we shared more than just an ordinary friendship, but she never said anything.

"Yeah, Alex is here. We're watching a movie." She took her phone out and handed it to me. It was an e-mail informing her that she had to do a mandatory course if she wanted to keep on helping out at the hospital. The course was in Chicago and would last a week. "I know it's the worst timing ever, but Alex can stay with you. I'm sure his parents won't mind. Let's ask him now." Without waiting for my response, she walked to my room and talked to Alex. I was still standing in the kitchen, processing.

Of course Mom and Alex planned everything. He would take me to the hospital to get tested and by the time we get the results, she'd probably be back home already. Alex's parents were okay with him staying with me, so everything was sorted. It was just me who worried. School would start soon and Elijah would be here. Alex would still be staying at my place and I very well knew that when it came to Alex, all bets were off. Despite everything, I was ecstatic about the fact that Alex would be sleeping over.

Mom left early the next morning. She came into my room and kissed me goodbye. "Take care of yourself, Honey. I'll call you when I land." I nodded and closed my eyes again. I was exhausted. It was like everything that has happened the past few weeks was finally catching up to me.

When I finally woke up, it was almost noon. I checked my phone and there was a message from Bev. She wanted an update on how things were going with me. I called and told her everything. I knew that she would be upset with me for not telling her sooner and for confiding in Alex instead, but I had to tell her eventually, so I ripped off the band aid.

As expected, Bev was pissed and even more so when I told her that Alex would be sleeping over until my mom returned home. "You're playing with fire, Hannah! I know you love Elijah and you want to be with him, so why do you keep throwing yourself at Alex?" I felt hurt by her words, but I knew she was right. I just couldn't seem to stay away from Alex.

"School will start soon and I'm sure when Elijah is here, I'll be able to let go of Alex a bit. So don't worry." Bev was silent for a while.

"Hannah, you'll get hurt and I'll have to be the one who picks up the pieces. Just be careful okay. I have to go."

I had just gotten out of the shower when someone knocked at the door. I thought it was Bev coming to yell at me in person, but when I opened the door, Alex was standing there with pizza and a bag filled with snacks. "Hi there. I thought we could go the hospital today and then have a movie night." I gave him a hug and his smell immediately made me want to kiss him.

"Sounds perfect. Let me just get my things then we can go." I was thankful that we could go to the hospital so soon. I wanted to get the test over with.

"How are you feeling about your dad and what he asked you to do?" His question caught me off guard. I actually wasn't sure how I felt about it.

"I mean, I am angry that he didn't even try to explain his absence or silence over the years before asking this huge thing from me, but I can't really expect more from the guy who abandoned his family now could I? And also, he is not my dad. He is just Dave."

At the hospital, before I got tested, the doctor thoroughly informed me about the procedure and the operation, should I be a match and decided to donate a kidney to Dave. He told me about the possible risks of surgery and also how having only one kidney could affect my life. As I listened to him list all the risks, I couldn't help but wonder whether Dave would do the same for me. Would he sacrifice a organ or even his life for me? Would he have even ever contacted me if it wasn't for his kidney failure? Does that man even love me? At the end of the day, the answers to these questions doesn't matter, because I would still be there, doing the test.

Chapter 10

Alex was sitting outside the hospital, patiently waiting on me. "I'm done. They said they will call with the results." He got up and gave me a hug.

"You are one amazing human, Hannah." The truth was that I was really proud of myself as well. I managed to put whatever I felt towards Dave aside and help him. It was something my mom would absolutely do. "Are you excited for the first day back at school tomorrow?" With everything else on my mind, I actually forgot that the next day was the first day of school.

"I actually forgot. Guess my mind has been all over the place lately." It was weird that I haven't heard from Bev yet. Usually she'd be at my place early the morning before the first day back at school to arrange our outfits, practice hairstyles and lecture me on how to wear make up. She was probably still mad at me about the whole Alex thing. Well, at least I wouldn't be alone. I had Alex.

When we pulled up in front of my house, the front door was open and I instantly knew it was Bev She knew where we kept the spare key and often used it when she came over and we weren't home. "Are your mom home already?" I could hear the disappointment in Alex's voice.

"No. I'm 100% sure its Bev." I said as I got out the car.

As expected, she already laid a bunch of outfits that she paired together on the bed. "Surprise!" She squealed and hugged me tight. "We're going to rock senior year my friend!" I was so relieved that she wasn't mad at me anymore, but also disappointed that I wouldn't spend the day alone with Alex.

"You're such a good friend Bev. Thank you." She looked at Alex with Disapproval written all over her face.

"It's going to be a very girly day , so I suggest you get yourself some movies or games or something to entertain yourself." Alex smiled and nodded. I could see he was also disappointed even though he tried to hide it.

Like always, Bev started experimenting hairstyles on me. I enjoyed it, even though I knew I'd never actually wear it like that. "So, how are you feeling about seeing Elijah tomorrow?" She sat down on the bed beside me.

"Of course I'm beyond excited. I missed him so much!" Bev smiled and I could tell she wanted to bring Alex up, so I decided to steer the conversation in another direction. "Lets talk about you. Who's hearts do you plan on breaking this year?" This topic was sure to keep her out of my love life for a while.

"Actually, I was thinking of having a monogamous relationship this year. With a boy who appreciate and accepts me for me." I was stunned. Bev never believed in monogamy. Guess she was growing up.

It was almost dark out when Bev left and Alex was in the kitchen preparing dinner. I liked the sight of him in the kitchen, wearing an apron and chopping onions. It made me want to jump him. Then I realized that we were alone. Nothing stood in my way of doing exactly that, so I walked toward him, took of my clothes and started kissing him. He also undressed and picked me up in his arms. I wrapped my legs around his waist. When we had sex, it was like everything around us were on fire, every time. I was overwhelmed with pleasure. Every inch of my body wanted every inch of his. I grabbed onto his biceps as I began to completely lose control of my body. I just surrendered my whole self to him and the pleasure he gave me.

My body was trembling while I got dressed. "I should take a shower before I finish dinner." I felt disappointed that he didn't invite me to join him, but I knew I had to calm my jets, especially since this probably was the last time we would be together like that.

"Yes, I'll go after you." I said, panting. While Alex was in the shower, I received a call from Elijah. He had arrived in Boston and was settling into the dorms. "I would love to see you, but I'm pretty tired from the long drive. Is it okay if I just see you tomorrow at school?" I was kind of relieved. I really didn't want to see Elijah just moments after I had sex with Alex.

"No problem. I'll see you tomorrow. Sweet dreams."

After dinner, we were watching a movie when Alex started the conversation I was afraid to have. "So, I guess tonight was the last time we had some benefit action huh?" He said it playfully, like it was no big deal to him, but I knew better. I knew that it was just as sad for him as it was for me. It would be very difficult to go back to just being friends.

"I guess so." I laid my head on his chest and continued watching the movie in silence.

The next morning, I woke up to the smell of coffee and croissants. Alex was already dressed and sipping on some coffee when I entered the kitchen. "Good morning. Thanks for making breakfast." He winked at me and gestured with his hand for me to sit down.

"Good morning Hannah. Do you want a ride to school?" Usually me and Bev would just walk to school, but on the first day, we always took a cab and I didn't want to upset her by suggesting we go with Alex.

"No thank you. Me and Bev have a tradition of taking a cab to school on the first day." Alex nodded and took a last sip of coffee before he got up. "I'll see you at school then. Have a great day Hannah." I wondered why he was heading out so early, but I didn't ask.

The outfit Bev set aside for me to wear was not my style at all. It was a pair of denim shorts, white sandals and a tight fitting white halter top. I had to admit though, I looked sizzling hot. I was excited for the new school year and being able to see Elijah everyday was going to be awesome. I smiled as I looked at myself in the mirror one last time before heading out. Bev was already outside, waiting in the cab. She looked gorgeous, as always. Finding a boyfriend wasn't going to be a problem for her at all.

Walking down the hall at school felt different. I felt different, good different. I was a senior and I was going to have a fabulous year with a fabulous boyfriend. I looked around for Elijah, but I couldn't see him anywhere. I turned around and there he was, talking to two girls I didn't recognize. He was even more cute than I remembered. I ran toward him and jumped in his arms. "Hannah! Hi... this is Tamlynn and Tamara. They are twins."

I was expecting an "I missed you" or "It's good to see you," or better yet, a kiss. "Hi girls. You guys also new?" I tried to hide the disappointment in my voice.

"Yeah. We're freshmen. Later Elijah." They walked away without even looking in my direction. Whatever. I wasn't going to let two little freshmen ruin my day. I turned my attention back to Elijah.

"How are you?" He looked distracted, but that was normal. He was in a new school, which is overwhelming.

"Hannah, can we talk later? I have to go." I'd be lying if I said that his behavior didn't sting. I decided not to read to much into it and went to class. To my surprise, Alex was there already.

"Come sit by me, friend." The way he said 'friend', I could tell he didn't believe it. Like it was just a joke.

I sat beside him and casually said: "Thank you friend." Just then the bell rang and kids flooded the classroom. I saw Elijah enter. He looked at me and then at Alex.

"I was hoping we'd sit together. Maybe in the next class?" He didn't wait for an answer. He just shot Alex a dirty look and then he walked to the back of the classroom.

"Guess your boyfriend's intimated by me." Alex smirked and satisfaction was written all over his face. The last thing I needed was a war between Alex and Elijah. Was Alex trying to make Elijah jealous? It was hard to believe that he would try to sabotage my relationship with Elijah on purpose, especially given the fact that he knew exactly how I felt about him.

It was lunch time already and I still haven't managed to be alone with Elijah. I was sitting in the cafeteria, when Elijah came and sat next to me. He kissed me on the cheek "Hi stranger. How about we grab a coffee after school?" I was relieved that he wanted to spend time with me.

"That would be awesome. I really missed you."

Chapter 11

We were meeting at the coffee shop just down the street from school. I was already waiting for ten minutes when he showed up, but he wasn't alone. Colin, Tamlynn and Tamara, the hot twins, was with him. Colin was known for the significant amount of girls he have hooked up with. He was a real player. I wasn't thrilled to see Elijah hanging out with them and even less so that he brought them along on our coffee date.

He kissed me on my cheek again. What was even up with that, I wondered. Then he whispered in my ear: "Sorry. They sort of invited themselves along." So, what was I supposed to do? I didn't even know what to say to them. It was awkward to say the least. Thankfully, my phone rang just as I opened my mouth to say something that was sure to be stupid. I excused myself and went outside to answer the call. It was the hospital and they had my test results. I hadn't expect the results to be ready so soon. I didn't even knew if I was ready.

"Hannah, would you like me to tell you now? Or do you prefer to come here and talk in person?" The doctor asked politely. What would be the point in waiting?

"Please just tell me now." I said. The silence on the other end felt like an eternity.

"Hannah, the results show that you are unfortunately not a match for your father. I'm very sorry." I suddenly felt numb. The realization that Dave would probably die, was accompanied by an unfamiliar emotion. All I knew was that I wanted to go home. I went back into the shop and told Elijah that I had to leave and bolted before he could even reply. I was pissed at him anyway.

Tears welled up in my eyes as the cab pulled up in front of my house. I didn't even understand why I wanted to cry. I barely knew the guy. I should be happy that I wouldn't have to get surgery, but instead I was overwhelmed with sadness. What was going on? I opened the front door and instinctively called out for Alex. He came out of the bathroom, wearing a towel around his waist. "Hannah what's wrong? You look upset." Seeing him was enough to make me burst out in tears. I allowed all the emotions to surface. I felt everything at once and collapsed in his arms. He held me tightly, not asking any questions. The only thing he said was: "I'm here."

After what felt like a lifetime, I finally managed to stop crying. "The hospital called and said that I wasn't a match for Dave. I feel so stupid for crying. I didn't even know the guy."

Alex placed his finger under my chin and lifted my face to his. "He is your father, Hannah and you are linked to him. Nothing can change that." He kissed my forehead and led me to my room.

"Now, rest a bit. I'll come check on you later, okay?" I nodded and closed my eyes, but I couldn't sleep. My thoughts were all over the place and I felt completely lost. I reached for my phone to check the time and saw a text from Elijah. *"Why did you bolt? Everything okay?"* Was this guy serious? I didn't have the strength to deal with him anyway. I sent my mom a text instead to tell her that I won't be able to safe her ex husband's life. I wanted to call Dave too, but I didn't know how to break the news to him. Maybe I could ask mom to tell him when she returned. I felt so drained. The day really kicked my ass. What a way to start my senior year. I didn't even get spend time alone with Elijah.

Alex knocked at the door and entered. He handed me a chocolate. "Hope you're feeling better." He was so sweet, but I couldn't help to think that it was Elijah's role he was playing. He was supposed to be the one to console me and bring me chocolate, but instead, he was hanging out with his new friends. I hoped that Alex wouldn't ask me about Elijah. I felt embarrassed that he didn't make more of an effort to be alone with me. Especially since we hadn't seen each other in such a long time. "I'll just order in tonight. Is that okay with you?"

Alex's words pulled me back to the present. "Yes. That'd be nice."

I was lying in the bathtub, surrounded by burning lavender candles and sipping on a cup of chamomile tea that Alex had made for me when my mom called. As expected, she wanted to come back home immediately. "Mom, please just finish your course. I had a momentary breakdown, but Alex supported and comforted me. I'm much better now." I knew she was worried about me, but I wanted her to complete the course.

"Honey, promise me that you'll tell me when you need me to come home okay? We can go to Portland when I return and tell Dave in person." The truth was that I didn't want to see Dave's face when he learns that he's going to die, but I didn't want to get into it over the phone.

"Okay mom. I love you."

When I came out of the bathroom, the smell of chinese food greeted me and I realized how hungry I was. Alex was in the living room, browsing through movies. "I thought we could watch a movie with dinner to preoccupy your mind." He was the best. That was exactly what I needed.

"Perfect!" I sat next to him on the carpet and helped myself to the food. He was unusually quiet, but I didn't mind. It was way better than talking about Dave or Elijah. "Thank you for everything." He smiled at me and continued watching the movie. I didn't wen know what movie it was and I didn't care. I was just thankful it killed the silence that lingered between us.

All I wanted to do was lay in his arms, but I knew that that would be playing with fire and considering the weird place me and Elijah was currently in, being close to Alex was going to be a big mistake. I wanted to get up, but he gently grabbed my arm. "Please stay. I would feel better if I could see you're okay." And just like that, all reason disappeared and I was playing with fire yet again. I climbed on top of him. He kissed me while unhooking my bra with his one hand. I completely surrendered to the craving of having him inside me. It was totally worth the burn.

It was clear that keeping our friendship free of sex, was damn near impossible. We couldn't resist each other and that wasn't fair towards Elijah. "Hannah, I have to tell you something." And then he uttered the six words that would change everything between us forever. The words I never expected to hear him say. "I am in love with you." It felt like my heart stopped beating and not in a good way. I couldn't speak or react in any other way for that matter. That was it. Our friendship was over. Hearing the vulnerability in his voice, made me want to cry.

"Alex, this was never supposed to be more than a friendship. I'm so sorry..." I looked up and saw hope dying in his eyes. I swear I could hear his heart breaking. It must've taken all his courage to confess and I had just shattered it all. I waited for him to say something, but he remained silent. I thought he would storm out, but he stayed. I thought he would be angry, but instead, he gave me a hug and then walked away.

I was laying in my bed, trying to make sense of the day, when Bev called. At first I didn't want to answer, but then I thought that I couldn't afford to lose the one friend I had left. "Bev, I had the worst day of my life." When I finished updating her on everything that happened that day, I expected her to yell at me for sleeping for Alex yet again and to tell me that it's my fault he got hurt, but instead all she said was:

"Damn babe, are you okay?" I wasn't. I bailed on Elijah without any explanation, let Dave down and broke Alex's heart. I was not okay. I was a terrible person.

The next morning, I woke up to Bev's voice. "Good morning sunshine!" She stood in my doorway with a coffee in her hand.

"Good morning. What are you doing here so early?" She came into my room and sat on the bed.

"Honey, Alex texted me last night and asked me to come stay with you until your mom comes back." I knew I didn't have the right to feel disappointed, but I couldn't help it. In my selfishness, I hoped that he would stay.

"You can say it. I am a special kind of asshole aren't I?" Bev burst out laughing.

"You're my asshole." She kissed me on my forehead and hugged me tightly. "Come on, get up and get ready. We have some damage control to do with Elijah."

Chapter 12

I managed to find Elijah easier than the day before. I walked up to him and kissed him on the cheek. "Sorry for bolting yesterday. The hospital called and I'm not a match for Dave." Just then the twins came along.

"Hi Elijah." Clearly I was invisible to these girls.

"Sorry guys. I really want to spend time alone with my girlfriend." I could see how jealousy consumed them when he took my hand and we walked away. He was finally acting like the guy I knew and loved. "I'm sorry Babe. That really sucks. What can I do to make you feel better?" Being with him like that was more than enough, but I was going to take advantage of the opportunity.

"Frozen yogurt after school?" He smiled and pulled me close.

"Done! I'll even throw in a kiss." He kissed me so passionately that, for a moment, I forgot we were at school.

The rest of the day, I was trying my best to avoid Alex, which wasn't too difficult, as he was doing the same. He didn't look my way once. I guess he hated me, but I couldn't blame him. I hated me too for breaking his heart. Elijah, on the other hand, was all over me every chance he got and I couldn't tell him to be more discreet with the public display of affection without him getting suspicious, so I just shoved my guilty feelings aside and enjoyed being in love.

After we got frozen yogurt, I invited Elijah to my place to catch up more privately. Bev had cheerleader practice, so we were alone and I was planning to take full advantage of the opportunity. I took him to my room and we started making out. The passion was high and I was ready to be with him and only him. So, we made love.

I laid on my bed, watching as he got dressed. His facial expression was hard to read. "How was it?" I wanted to hear him say how amazing it was and how I rocked his world.

"It was good, Hannah. Thank you." I was shocked. Good? What did that even mean? And "Thank you?" What was going on in his head?

I tried not to fixate on his words too much, but I was having trouble and before I could help myself, the words flew out of my mouth: "What does that even mean?" I sounded offensive and it was too late to take it back.

"Okay. It was great. Really great. And I was just thanking you for an amazing time." He playfully pinched my cheek and then checked his phone. "I should get going. See you tomorrow?" I was hoping he'd hang out a bit longer, but I wasn't going to risk sounding desperate too, so I just nodded.

"See you tomorrow."

As soon as he left, I wanted to call Alex, but I couldn't. I missed him so much. He was easy to be with - no drama. With him, what you saw was what you got. Elijah, on the other hand, was the definition of complicated. I liked challenges, just not when it involved the boy I was in love with. The harsh truth was that I messed up things with Alex, maybe beyond repair and now it felt like I was heading down the same road with Elijah too. And if that wasn't enough, Dave was also lingering in the back of my mind. I needed some comfort.

I was busy making burgers for dinner when Bev arrived home. "Hi. How was your date?" I felt bad for always dumping all my drama on her. I wasn't the only person in our friendship.

"Oh never mind that. How are you? How was practice?" Bev looked at me funny, but then she went into "me-mode" and squealed.

"Guess who asked me out? Colin!" This was the same Colin that Elijah were hanging out with, the biggest player in school. I wanted to warn Bev, but I also didn't want to put a damper on her excitement, so I just hugged her.

"I'm happy you're happy." And it was the truth. Besides, should shit hit the fan, which was bound to happen, I'd be there for her, just like she'd always been there for me.

It was finally Friday which meant that my mom would be home soon. I really needed her to hold me and tell me that everything was going to be okay. Unwillingly, I got out of bed. Going to school was the last thing I wanted to do, but unfortunately I didn't have the luxury of skipping as I needed to maintain a perfect record if I wanted to get accepted into Harvard the following year. I haven't told anyone that that's where I wanted to go yet, not even my mom. Maybe it was because on some level I didn't think I'd ever get in. I mean it was Harvard, after all.

I put on my black wide leg pants and a yellow top that Bev once gave me for my birthday. Bev made a delicious breakfast, but coffee was all I could stomach . I was stressed out. The week was nerve-wracking and I just wanted it to be over. Bev was talking about the senior sleepover which was a tradition where all seniors slept on the football field in sleeping bags after making a bonfire and secretly getting drunk, and hooking up. Of course Bev was super excited to go, but I would be perfectly happy staying home and watching a movie from the comfort of my own bed. Hopefully in Elijah's arms.

"Hannah! I'm talking to you!" I was so lost in my own thoughts that I didn't hear half of what she said. "I'm sorry Bev, but I think I'd rather watch a movie with Elijah in the privacy of my room." She rolled her eyes and handed me a muffin. "Whatever. You can eat that on the go. We're going to be late." I was in no hurry to get to school, but Bev grabbed my hand and practically ran out the house. Thankfully, she ordered us a cab to school.

We were already halfway through the day when I were able to speak to Elijah alone for the first time. He was surrounded by his friends all the time. "So, senior sleepover sounds like fun huh? Can I squeeze into your sleeping bag?" He whispered in my ear and kissed my neck. I felt flustered almost immediately. "Sounds great, but I was actually hoping we could spend some time together. Maybe watch a movie in my room...alone." I could see the disapproval on his face. He wanted to go to the sleep over. No doubt.

"Hannah, this is our senior year. It only comes around once, hopefully. We should be experiencing all the senior year traditions and I really want to do that with you." How could I refuse an offer like that? I would go to the moon with him if he asked me to. "How could I say no to that?" He picked me up in his arms and twirled me around until I squealed.

Finally, it was the last period of the day. Unfortunately, it was the class where Alex sat next to me. Lately, he tried everything to avoid speaking to me and although it hurt, I couldn't blame him. I just really missed him. In more ways than one. Alex made me feel things that I just don't feel with Elijah. It's not that I was comparing them, it was just a painfully undeniable fact. "You going to the sleep over, Alex?" It was Lisa. She was not exactly known for her shy and sweet personality. 'Wild' was the only word I would use to describe her and she was definitely not Alex's type at all.

"Yeah sure." He said and winked at her. What was that I just felt? Jealousy? Seriously? I wanted to slap myself across the face. She asked for his phone and typed something on it. It could only be her number. I was sure of it. How could she behave so cheaply? It was girls like them who gave us all a bad name. I tried to compose myself, because I had no right to judge her or anyone else for that matter. If hanging out with Lisa would make him happy, then I'd be happy for him.

The bell rang, putting an end to my thoughts about Alex and Lisa. I could go home and hold my mom and everything would be better. I hastily jumped up from my seat and headed for the door, but as fate would have it, I tripped and landed with my face flat on the floor. "Hannah! are you okay?" I felt someone wrapping their arms around my waist and lifting me up. I expected it to be Elijah, but it was Alex. "Your mouth is bleeding. Are you okay?" Just then Elijah appeared and held my face in both his hands.

"I'll take it from here. Thanks man." He didn't even look at Alex once.

"Thank you Alex." My voice sounded unstable, like I was crying. He didn't say anything back, just nodded and walked away.

"Come on, let's get you cleaned up." Elijah took my hand and led me to the school nurse.

I can't describe the happiness that filled me when I saw my mom's car parked in the driveway of our house when I got home. I couldn't get inside the house soon enough. I called out her name urgently. "Mom!" I ran into her arms and started crying. I held onto her for dear life. I succumbed to the heartache I tried to suppress and became the most vulnerable version of myself in my mom's arms.

After what felt like an eternity crying, I finally calmed down and was able to talk to her. "Hannah, remember it's always darkest before the dawn." She took both my hands in hers. "We can go see Dave tomorrow. Okay?"

She didn't know about the other things that also happened. Maybe it was time I told her. "Mom, there's something else I want to tell you." I told her everything about Elijah and Alex, well, not every detail, just enough for her to understand how I was feeling.

"I'm so sorry I wasn't here for you, Honey. It sounds like it's been a rough week for you." It was mind-blowing how just being in her presence, made everything seem so much better. "I'll make us some tea and then we can continue catching up."

Mom made tea and sandwiches. I didn't even realize how hungry I was until I saw it. "So, Hannah, I don't want to tell you what to do, but I'd like to tell you what I'm thinking. Will that be okay?" I took a sip of my tea and nodded. I always appreciated my moms input and advice. She was my mom after all, she knew me best. "Honey, I think that deep down, subconsciously maybe, you are in love with Alex. You shared so much with him. It's obvious that you trust him more." She probably saw the shock on my face and that's why she immediately added: "That said, I know you and you will never hurt someone on purpose. You have your reasons. Just please promise me that you'll never settle for anything less than what you deserve." I knew she meant well, but honestly, she somehow managed to confuse me all over again.

Chapter 13

My mom suggested that we go see Dave the next day and even though it would be better to do it sooner, rather than later, it was still a very heavy task to execute. I called Bev and invited her to go with us. I wanted to include her more and I also wanted as much support as I could get.

While I was digging through my closet to find something comfortable to wear, I found a hoodie that Alex loaned me one night. We were watching a movie at his house and as usual with us, one thing led to another and we totally lost track of time. It was already dark out and very chilly when I was heading home, so he gave me the hoodie to wear. It still smelled like him. I embraced it and then put it on. It was almost like I was hugging him. Oh how I wished to be in his arms.

I crawled into bed, still wearing the hoodie and grabbed my phone to text him: *"Alex, I really miss you. Please come over?"* I honestly wasn't expecting a reply, so when I didn't hear anything from him a few minutes later, I turned off the light and closed my eyes, embracing the hoody. Suddenly, my phone rang. It was Alex. I picked up hesitantly. "Hannah, I'm outside your house." I was still trying to figure out how he went from not talking to me, to waiting for me in front of my house in just a few hours when I reached his car. He was standing outside, holding the passenger door open for me.

He didn't speak, just gestured for me to get in. "What's up, Hannah?" He sounded so nonchalant, like we were just acquaintances. I didn't even know how to answer his question.

"Well, I'm seeing Dave tomorrow to break the news to him." He wiped his face with his hands like he was trying to calm himself. "I can just imagine how difficult this is for you. I'm really sorry Hannah." I couldn't help to wonder whether he was apologizing because he won't be there for me or just because it was the decent thing to do.

"I came across your hoodie in my closet earlier tonight. It made me miss you terribly. Alex, won't you please forgive me and be part of my life again?"

I wasn't at all prepared for what he said next. "How could you be so selfish? You broke my heart, Hannah. Unless you want all of me, you can't get any part of me. I can't be just your friend anymore." Tears welled up in his eyes and then he said something that really shook me to my core. "He will hurt you. I know he will. He doesn't realize your worth." He looked me in the eyes and gently tucked my hair behind my ear. "I don't think I'll ever completely get over you, but I refuse to be your consolation anymore."

I didn't know what to say. I felt so guilty for being the root of his despair. He deserved better. "I'm sorry Alex. I'll do my best to let you go. Just know that no one will ever take your place in my heart." And with that, I kissed him on his cheek, got out of his car and walked away without looking back. I was finally letting him go.

As I closed the front door behind me, I also closed the chapter of me and Alex. The searing pain in my chest was undeniable. As I was sitting on the floor of my bedroom, I cried for the loss of my very special friend and I knew in my bones that I'd never be the same person again. I just lost my favorite person.

I didn't even knew how and when I fell asleep that night. When I woke up the next morning, there was an intense emptiness in my heart. I couldn't wrap my head around the fact that Alex was no longer in my life, but I had to shove that sadness aside. There was another sad situation I had to deal with that day. I had to tell Dave that I couldn't help him and that he was probably going to die. It seemed like all I did was hurt people around me and that really sucked.

Bev was lying in the back of the car, Mom was humming along to a country song and I was hiding behind some very large sunglasses to avoid questions about my swollen eyes. The drive to Portland felt excruciatingly long. Probably because I wanted the whole nightmare to be over and done with as soon as possible.

It felt like a lifetime ago when I was sitting on the beach in Massachusetts. Everything was so simple. There were no boys in my life; Bev was my only friend, and I was still a virgin. How did everything get so complicated? In that moment I wished I could be in Massachusetts again, standing on the beach, allowing the ocean to heal me. Instead, I was on my way to tell Dave that I couldn't save his life after I broke the heart of someone special to me the night before.

We drove past the "Welcome to Portland" sign, and my heart started pounding in my chest. It felt like I was about to have an anxiety attack, so I put my head between my legs and took deep breaths to calm myself. I felt a hand on my back and I knew it was Bev comforting me. I was so grateful that she came along. She had her flaws, but when I needed her, she was always there, no questions asked.

My head was spinning with all the mixed thoughts and emotions, when I needed to focus only on one thing - Dave. As mom parked the car, tears welled up in my eyes. "Hannah, you don't have to come in with me. You can just wait here." I really wanted to take her up on her offer, but it could've been the last time I'd saw him and I needed to say my peace and hopefully get closure.

"No mom. I'm coming with you." We got out the car and Bev hugged me.

"You are the bravest person I know Hannah. I'm so proud of you."

As we entered the hospital, I could feel my courage fading and fear surfacing. I clung onto every ounce of strength I had inside me and kept on walking until I reached Dave's room. I stopped abruptly, realizing that I didn't have the words to deliver the worse news of his life to him. Like she could read my mind, my mom whispered reassuringly: "don't be afraid. I'll do all the talking." She held my hand as we entered his room, but he wasn't alone. His family were there too. Everyone stopped talking and all eyes were on us as we approached Dave.

"Hi everyone. Dave, how are you feeling?" Mom was so calm and even though no one greeted her back, she remained poised. I could only hope that I'd one day have her strength.

"Hannah, do you have good news?" The audacity of that man stunned me. What did mom even saw in him? He was just awful. Mom took a deep breath and then broke the news to him.

"Hannah got tested, but unfortunately she isn't a match for you. We are so deeply sorry, Dave." He covered his face with his hands and I wasn't sure that I could handle seeing him cry. I was contemplating leaving the room, when he suddenly started shouting.

"You good for nothing girl! The one thing I ask of you and you can't even do that! You and your mom are both useless! You are no child of mine!"

It took me a while to phantom the hurtful words that were coming out of his mouth. I looked around the room at his family and then I walked closer to him, looked him in his eyes and said: "I forgive you. May God have mercy on your soul." I slowly backed away and then the most unexpected thing happened.

My mom slapped him so hard across his face, I thought he might cry. "Rest in peace you miserable bastard." I was beyond shocked. She took my hand and we walked out. Bev was standing right outside the room with her hand covering her mouth. Of course she watched the whole thing. I wasn't even surprised. "Way to go Aunt Addy!" she said loud and proudly. And that was it – another chapter closed.

I wanted to text Alex. I don't think I ever wanted anything so badly before, but I had to stay away. Even though I couldn't give him what he wanted, I could still give him my respect.

The next few days were a blur as I was recovering from the traumatic experience I had with Dave. I was grieving for the loss of the father I never had – as far as I was concerned, he was dead already. I would never get the closure I wanted, the apology I was entitled to and the love from him I deserved.

I haven't heard from Alex since the night he told me to let him go and watching him from a distance was agonizing. Luckily I had Bev to cheer me up with junk food and Elijah to distract me with super hot make out sessions.

Time seemed to fly by and soon it was time to start filling out college applications. I had decided to apply to Harvard, Yale and Columbia. They had the best literature programs, which was what I decided to study. After I submitted my applications, I felt like celebrating, so I invited Bev to go shoe shopping. "Bev, I applied to Harvard, Yale and Columbia today. Have you applied to colleges yet?" She looked surprised, and understandably so.

"That's awesome Hannah! We should celebrate! I also submitted my applications yesterday."

She picked up some cute pink sneakers and handed it to me. "These are year style and its your size too.!" She was right – I absolutely loved it. "And these are perfect for me!" She pointed to a pair of flaming red pumps with a glitter belt in the middle. It was over the top and exactly her style.

The night of the senior sleepover, Elijah offered to pick me and Bev up at my house. It was the perfect opportunity to introduce him to my mom. "It's a pleasure to meet you Miss Clark." My mom smiled and shook his hand.

"It's nice to meet you too Elijah and please, just call me Addison or Addie." Bev burst out laughing, just like I knew she would. She was enjoying seeing Elijah so nervous.

"Relax dude. Aunt Addie is one of the coolest grown ups I know." I grabbed my overnight bag and kissed mom on the cheek.

When we arrived on the football field, most of the seniors were there already. It was like a party, everyone was talking and laughing. The vibe was amazing. I searched for Alex in the crowd and saw him standing next to Lisa. And there it was again, the jealousy burning in my stomach. Our eyes met for just a second and it was absolute torture to pretend like everything was fine, like I was fine. I walked over to where Elijah was talking to Colin and some other girls. "Hi babe" I kissed him, but he pulled away.

"Babe, we're not alone." He said abruptly. I felt humiliated and lashed out saying that he wasn't the same person I fell in love with. He looked at me judgingly, which sent me off the edge.

"You know what, I'm sick of your hot and cold games. Call me when your PMS is over." I yelled and walked away. I noticed that all eyes were on me, but at that moment, I couldn't care less. Bev handed me a drink.

"Don't worry babe. You spoke your truth. The ball is in his court now." I took the drink and practically inhaled it.

"Another one please." I asked. Bev didn't say anything, she just handed me her drink instead. I kept on pounding down one drink after the other while I danced around the bonfire with Bev. I was dancing and singing along to one of my favorite songs when I bumped into someone. It was Alex. Even though I was tipsy, I still felt the electricity of our touch, but each touch we shared was a painful reminder that we could never be us again.

He looked at me worried . "You should take it easy Hannah." Before I could reply, Bev pulled me away and shoved another drink in my hand. She held her red cup in the air and said proudly.

"Screw boys! We don't need them, because we'll always have each other!" And that's the last thing I remember of that night.

Chapter 14

I woke up with a massive hangover the next morning. Served me right for making such an unnecessary scene the previous night, I thought to myself. The part I was most upset about, was that Alex saw how obnoxiously I handled the situation. I didn't even want to know what he thought of me.

Bev woke up while I was gathering my things. "I'm calling us a cab. Let's get out of here" I whispered as not to wake the others.

"Hannah, I'm going home first. I need a shower and some sleep." Bev sounded agitated. I thought that it was probably just a result of the hangover that was kicking my ass too.

The cab arrived and as we got in, I asked Bev go with me to my house instead so we could puzzle out the events of the previous night together, but she looked at me like I was speaking a unfamiliar language.

"You can't seriously be this selfish Hannah. All we talk about these days are you and your problems. I'm fed up and hung over." I was taken aback by her words, but I understood where she was coming from.

I began to apologize , but Bev held her hand up in the air and interrupted me. "Just please stop. I need to get of the Hannah–roller-coaster. I'm done!" She turned to the cab driver and asked him to pull over so she could get out. I was stunned, but truth be told, Bev was right - I've been selfish. The past few months was all about me and my life. I felt nauseated by the realization of my oblivious egocentrism.

Mom wasn't home, so I went straight to the bathroom. Standing in the shower, I closed my eyes and imagined that the water was washing all my troubles away. I savored the feeling of the water flowing over my body. It reminded me of when Alex used to touch me – every single part of my body. I was suddenly overwhelmed by an urgent urge to have him close to me, inside me. Fighting against every fiber in me that wanted to call him, I forced myself to rather think about how to fix things with Elijah instead.

After putting on my sweatpants and a t-shirt, I made myself some tea in the hope of gaining clarity. I replayed the drama of the previous night over and over in my mind until I finally puzzled out that I was wrong. I was the one who humiliated Elijah in front of everyone.

My phone rang and I was surprised to see it was Elijah. "Hi babe. I was just thinking about you." I tried to sound as sweet as possible.

"Hi Hannah. We need to talk. Can I come over?" I agreed even though I was terrified that he might want to break up. As I downed the last of my beverage, I tried not to jump to conclusions, but I struggled to shift my thoughts.

Standing in front of Elijah, I realized that I hadn't changed. My hair was tied in a messy bun and I still had my sweats on.

"Elijah, I'm so sorry. I have no excuse for my poor behavior." I didn't look at him. I didn't want him to see me cry when he broke up with me.

"Hannah, I should be apologizing to you. I haven't been treating you right. You deserve better." I was caught off guard by his apology. It was the last thing I expected, but instead of feeling happy, I felt uneasy, like I was waiting for the other shoe to drop. Was it supposed to be that easy? Did I really deserve this kindness after treating him so badly? Either he was an angel or I was missing something.

He brought me back to reality when he kissed me. I could feel how much he wanted me by the way he held me. I led him to my room and he pushed me against the closed door and continued kissing me while his hands caressed my breasts. It felt so good.

He then picked me up and laid me down on the bed. We made love, passionate and incredible love. I realized it was true what they say about make up sex. As we laid in my bed, breathless, I felt grateful that I could call the most amazing guy in the world my boyfriend.

"How about we go for a walk and I buy you some ice cream?" He suggested and for the first time in a long time, he was the guy I fell in love with, in fact, he was even better.

We had the most amazing day and I wanted to share every detail of it with my best friend, but I was too nervous to call her. Things had never been that bad between us before. Sure, we've argued, but this time was different. I called her even though I knew the chances of her picking up were slim to none, but miraculously, she answered. I was both thrilled and surprised. "Hi Hannah." I couldn't quite tell by the tone of her voice whether she was still mad or not.

"Hi Bev. I really want to apologize to you. I had been a terrible friend and if you'll give me a second chance, I promise I'll be better." I pleaded sincerely.

"I was too hard on you. You're just human after all. I'm sorry too, but I think we need some time apart. Okay?" Life without Bev seemed unbearable, even if it was just for a while, but I had to respect her wishes.

"I understand. Take as much time as you need." I said, feeling defeated.

The next two weeks were excruciating without my bestie. We still acted civil towards each other and made small talk, but it wasn't the same and I missed how we used to be.

Each day I had to fight the urge to call or text her, it was torture not being able to talk to her or see her when I wanted. We've been friends for so long that it was weird not seeing her everyday.

I wondered whether being apart was just as difficult for her as it was for me. I already lost Alex, I couldn't lose Bev too.

I decided to call her, but she didn't pick up. I felt so hopeless, but I wasn't going to give up that easily, so I texted her. *"Hi Bev. I miss you so much. Can we please be friends again?"* Three hours had passed and I still haven't heard from her.

I had a chemistry assignment that was due the next day, but I was struggling to focus. I opened my laptop to give it another try and then I saw an e-mail from Harvard. They invited me for a weekend-visit to explore the campus. I was overjoyed and practically leaped to my mom where she was cooking dinner in the kitchen. When I shared the good news with her, she squealed and hugged me tightly. "My Hannah, you're growing up too fast." I could see tears welling up in her eyes and I kissed her on the cheek.

"Don't worry, Mom. I'll always be your baby." The weekend-visit was in a month and I hoped that Bev and me would be back to being friends by then. We could explore the campus together , maybe even go to a dorm party and meet other students. I knew it was wishful thinking, but I comforted myself that anything was possible.

The next day at school, I saw Alex hanging out with Lisa again. Every time I saw them together, I was filled with jealousy. She didn't deserve his friendship. I just knew she didn't appreciate him like he deserved. To her, he was just another conquest she could brag to her friends about. I reminded myself that it wasn't my business and I didn't have the right to have an opinion on his life anymore.

I searched for Elijah in the crowd and saw him and Bev talking. She saw me approaching them, then quickly walked away. The fact that she didn't even wanted to be in my presence, broke my heart. I made my way to Elijah and he hugged me. I couldn't hold back my tears anymore. "Hannah, please don't me a scene. People will think I'm the one making you cry. "He said irritated, while looking around him. I was so disgusted by his behavior that the tears immediately stopped. His hot and cold routine was really getting to me.

"Whatever Elijah." I said and walked away.

I was reading a prescribed poem in class, when Alex walked past me. His hand lightly grazed mine. His touch instantly awoken a fire inside me and I looked up to see whether he felt it too, but he just kept walking to the back of the class. For the first time, I wondered whether I made a mistake in choosing Elijah over Alex. At least with Alex I knew exactly where I stood and he never hurt me. I shook my head like that would help get the thoughts out of my mind and continued reading the poem in front of me.

I felt my repressed emotions surfacing as I walked home. The agony was getting unbearable and I needed my best friend. I pulled out my phone and called Bev – of course she didn't answer. My vision was blurred by the tears welled up behind my eyelids. I suddenly realized that she might be more forgiving if I went to her house and spoke to her in person. Her house was just around the corner and before long, I was knocking at her front door. There was no answer. I took a deep breath before entering the house, but nothing could've prepared me for the scorching pain my heart was about to endure.

I heard noises coming from the kitchen. As I got closer, I realized that it was sex noises. Stunned, I stood there, not sure what to do. The decent thing would've been to turn around and exit the house quietly, but an indescribable feeling urged me to keep moving forward. "That's it...right there." Bev's voice was filled with pleasure. Softly, I walked into the kitchen and saw them having wild and passionate sex. She was sitting on the counter with her back arched while he was standing between her widely spread legs. Again, she let out a groan while he rapidly thrust in and out of her.

"Elijah?" I whispered. He somehow heard me through the grunting and instantly backed away from Bev. For several moments there was absolute silence. I swear I could hear my heart pounding in my chest.

"The best friend and the boyfriend. What a cliché." I said, trembling as tears filled my eyes, but I held them at bay. I refused to let them see me cry, so I raced outside.

"Hannah! Please wait!" Elijah called from inside the house. Without looking back, I sprinted without a destination in mind, trying to make sense of what I had just witnessed.

After what felt like a lifetime of running, I stopped to catch my breath. The sound of Bev moaning kept playing over and over in my mind. I gradually became aware of my surroundings and realized that I was near Alex's house, but I couldn't even go to him for solace. Dispirited, I slowly walked home.

Chapter 15

I got under the covers as soon as I was in my room. My heart was shattered by two people I loved immensely and I had no idea how I would come back from that. I unlocked my phone and saw a bunch of missed calls from both Bev and Elijah. Just then, the phone rang. It was Alex. Bewildered, I answered the call. "Hi Alex."

"Hannah, are you okay? Where are you?" He sounded frantic and I wondered if something bad had happened.

"I'm home. What's wrong?" My heart started thumping from anxiety. I couldn't deal with more bad news.

"I'll be right there." He hung up before I could ask any more questions. I glanced at myself in the mirror. My eyes were swollen and bloodshot. Heartache was written all over my face. In that moment I wished that I had some make-up so Alex wouldn't see me like that. I brushed my hair and tied it into a ponytail before I headed outside.

As usual, he was holding the passenger side door of his car open for me. I could feel his eyes on me, but I didn't look at him. When he got into the car, I suddenly felt overwhelmed with mixed emotions, which made it hard to breath. I rolled down the window and closed my eyes as the cool air touched my face. "Hannah, Bev called me. She told me what happened and they wanted to make sure that you are okay." How the hell could they possibly think that I would be okay and how could Alex even utter such ridiculous words. I couldn't bring myself so speak. "Hannah...."

That's all he said. Just Hannah. The silence between us was filled with unspoken words and I couldn't hold back the tears anymore and they fell from my eyes, continuously and silently. He gently lifted my chin and looked me in the eyes. "He doesn't deserve you Hannah. Please don't cry." His voice was like medicine for my broken heart.

"You warned me, Alex. You said that he would break my heart." He gently wiped my tears with the back of his hand. "The twisted truth is that I still love them even though they so viciously ripped out my heart." I said and laid my head on his shoulder.

I spent the next week isolated from everything and everyone. At school I avoided Bev and Elijah and at home, I spent all my time alone in my room, watching movies, eating chocolates and crying my eyes out.

Alex texted me occasionally to check how I was doing, but we hadn't seen each other since that horrible day.

It turned out that the time I spent alone gave me clarity. I've realized that life is precious, and I refused to waste any more of my time and energy on hating them. Although the anger and heartache remained, and my heart was still broken, I made the conscious decision not to let it destroy me.

I called Elijah without a clear idea of what I wanted to say. "Hannah?" Hearing his voice felt like a knife piercing through my chest.

Summoning all my strength, I spoke, "Elijah, I need you to keep quiet and listen. What you and I had was beautiful until it wasn't. Now, we are nothing but a tragedy. You shattered us along with my heart. I may forgive you someday, but for now, please stay away from me. Goodbye." I hung up and broke down in tears. I truly loved that blue-eyed boy.

My mind drifted back to the day we met; it felt like a lifetime ago. How could he changed so drastically in such a short time? Or was he wearing a mask all along, and I was too blind to see it?

Breaking up with Elijah was a difficult decision, but one I was certain about. Bev, on the other hand, was a different story. I had known her for so long; she was practically family. I didn't know if I could or even wanted to erase her from my life. However, whenever I saw her, all I could see was the one who had betrayed me with my boyfriend. I knew I wouldn't be able to talk to her without breaking down, so I decided to send her a text. *"Bev, I've been trying to understand how and why you could hurt me so badly. You betrayed me in the worst possible way and didn't even have the decency to apologize. Out of respect for our years of friendship, I forgive you. However, you are not my friend anymore; you are nothing to me. You will reap what you sow. – Hannah"*

I had just changed into my pajamas when I received a text from Alex: *"Hi Hannah. Fancy catching a movie? I'm outside."* It seemed like Alex and I were finally on our way to being friends again. This time, I was determined that we'd remain just friends. I texted him back: *"I'm already my pajamas. Get some snacks and come inside. We can watch a movie here."* I knew that inviting him in was a daring move, especially with my mom working a night shift at the hospital, but going out was the last thing I wanted to do.

A few minutes later, Alex arrived with chocolates, popcorn and biscuits. I wanted to hug him, but instead, I just thanked him for the snacks. "So, Hannah, what rom-com are you torturing me with tonight?" For the first time in a while, I genuinely laughed.

"How about we watch a horror or suspense movie instead? You can pick the first one." I settled onto the couch, covering myself with a blanket in anticipation. Alex put on a horror and I instantly regretted not opting for a rom-com instead. The opening music of the movie send shivers down my spine.

"Would you like some popcorn?" Alex held out the bowl to me from his spot on the couch across from me. I wasn't really a fan of popcorn - it always made me choke.

"Can I have chocolate instead, please?" I asked. He shook his head and smiled, handing me the chocolates. The movie was nerve-wracking, but interesting. It revolved around a woman whose husband cheated on her after twenty years of marriage. Upon discovering his affair, she was determined to seek revenge at all costs.

"Don't go getting any ideas, Hannah," Alex joked, munching on some biscuits.

"If I wanted revenge, they would both be gone by now," I replied. The shocked look on his face was priceless and I burst out laughing. Being around him made me so happy.

"You're such a dork!" He teasingly pulled on my ponytail and before I knew it, I was sitting on his lap, kissing him. I didn't even think about it. It was like my body had a mind of its own. He gently pushed me away.

"Hannah, I can't get my heart broken again. Losing you almost killed me." His words struck me like a slap across the face.

"Alex, I want you. It'll always be you, I'll always choose us." It felt like I was blind and suddenly, I could see, amazed at what I'd been missing.

"Hannah, you just made me the happiest guy alive." He pulled me closer and kissed me. I didn't think that our kisses could be more passionate and intense than before, but it was. He was mine and I was his. We made love like never before. It was amazing, magical even.

Chapter 16

After a long time, I was happy again. Things between Alex and I were going great. He had somehow healed my broken heart and filled it with joy. While I still missed Bev, I had learned to adapt to her absence in my life. It was difficult to understand how I could simultaneously miss and resent her though.

As I sat on the porch, enjoying a refreshing glass of juice, a text from Alex lit up my phone. *"Sweetheart, I have a surprise for you. Pack your bags. We're going away for the weekend. Don't forget your bikini."* Excited, I rushed into the house, interrupting my mom while she was working on her laptop.

"Mom, Alex wants to take me on a weekend trip," I said, unsure if it was a question or a statement.

She smiled warmly and replied: "Yes, Honey, he asked for my permission a week ago. It's all good. Just remember be stay safe." I hugged her tightly before heading off to my room to pack. I tossed some clothes and my bikini into a suitcase, excited for the adventure ahead.

We had been driving for about an hour when Alex told me that we were going to Massachusetts. He must have seen the hesitation on my face, because he gently touched my hand and said, "Hannah, remember I told you not to let Elijah take your happy place from you? It's yours, and I'm taking you there so we can share in happiness together." And just like that, I felt light-hearted again. I was going to make memories with Alex, magical memories that I'd cherish forever.

"You have no idea how much this means to me, Alex," I said, resting my hand on his thigh. He gave me a mischievous look, and I knew exactly what he wanted to do because it was precisely what I yearned for too.

"Control yourself, Alex. We have the whole weekend to be naughty," I said teasingly. He smiled widely, and I couldn't help but smile back. I turned on the radio and closed my eyes while I reminisced about the times we had shared together. From the moment we first spoke and there we were, madly in love with each other. Like a puzzle, we just fit, period.

As we drove into Massachusetts, I rolled down my window and let the ocean breeze tousle through my hair. "Oh, Alex, do you feel that? I'm home again." I said, excited for the magical experiences that awaited us.

"Hannah, I love you so much." I turned to him and saw the affection in his eyes. It made me wonder how I got so lucky as to fall in love with my best friend.

"I love you too. Always. Never forget that." I replied overwhelmed with gratitude.

"We're here." He pulled up into the driveway of a luxurious-looking guest house with the most gorgeous view of the ocean.

"Is this where we're staying?" I asked, amazed by the beauty surrounding me.

"Yes, it is. You should see the inside." Alex unloaded our luggage and made his way inside the building. "You coming?" He asked looking at me over his shoulder.

"Ill be right there." I said, then I faced the ocean and took a moment to appreciate it all. The smell of the ocean, the wind through my hair and the sound of the waves.

Alex was spot on. The interior of the guest house was exquisite, with a mixture of olive green and gold décor. The air was filled with the scent of lavender and jazz music was playing softly. The receptionist greeted Alex enthusiastically, completely overlooking me in the process. "Hi there, Cutie, how may I help you?" Her obvious flirting with him right in front of me was unsettling.

"Excuse me, Miss, could you kindly refrain from flirting with my boyfriend?" I asked sarcastically, and Alex couldn't help but let out a chuckle, trying to hide his grin.

The receptionist's face turned red as she quickly handed me a set of keys. "You're in room 8," she stated abruptly, avoiding my gaze. I accepted the keys with a satisfied smile, while Alex seemed amused by the situation.

A butler in a black suit approached us graciously. "Good day and welcome. May I assist you with your luggage and show you to your room?" His friendly demeanor and helpful offer instantly won me over. When he opened the door to the room, I was amazed. The décor, the carpet, the bedding, and curtains, the en-suite bathroom – everything was beautiful. But the most stunning feature was the jacuzzi on the balcony, with a view overlooking the ocean. I knew Alex's parents were wealthy, but I never expected luxury like this. Alex tipped the butler and closed the door.

He pulled me close, kissing me passionately. His touch still had the power to make me weak in the knees. He laid me down on the bed and slowly undressed me, building up the anticipation. My body was trembling with desire. He kissed my neck, my chest, my breasts gently.

"Alex...please," I gasped.

"Do you want me, Hannah?" I nodded. "Say it," he urged in a husky voice.

"I want you, Alex...please..." I wanted every part of him, the good and the bad, both physically and emotionally. I gave myself to him completely – heart, body, and soul. We were intertwined on every level, a bond that could never be broken.

The next morning, I woke up feeling content in every way, wrapped in Alex's arms. The aroma of coffee and freshly baked pastries made me realize how hungry I was. Slowly, I turned around and kissed Alex on his forehead. "Wake up sleepy head," I said softly. He opened his eyes and smiled.

"I could get used to waking up next to you, Hannah." He said, stroking his hand against my cheek.

"Lets go get breakfast. I'm famished," I said as I got out of bed. "I'll go shower first. It's probably safer that way – otherwise we'll never leave this room."

Alex laughed as he got up "I can't argue with that. Go ahead, I'll wait for you."

I blew him a kiss and headed to the bathroom. I decided to wear a white sundress with a golden belt and sandals. After curling my hair and putting on some lip gloss, I felt satisfied with my appearance and left the bathroom. "Wow!!!" Alex whistled and twirled me around. "How am I supposed to keep my hands to myself with you looking like that?"

"Okay, stop exaggerating and get your cute butt in the shower." I said teasingly.

I decided to call my mom while I waited, but she didn't answer, so I sent her a text: *"Hi Mom. How are you? Everything is beautiful here. We're about to get breakfast and then head out for the day. Love you. Hannah."*

Later, we enjoyed a breakfast buffet downstairs where I had blueberry muffins, a fruit salad and coffee, while Alex had eggs, bacon, toast, and sausage. "Wow! Are you really that hungry?" I asked in disbelief. He joked about needing energy after our night together, making me blush. As we discussed our plans to visit Aunt Lillian, do some sightseeing, and watch the sunset on the beach, Alex mentioned the possibility of her asking about Bev. I considered telling her the truth about our friendship ending, but not all the details.

I savored the last sip of my coffee, while Alex devoured every last bite of his breakfast. "Ready to go?" I asked, feeling excited to see Aunt Lillian again. Alex nodded as he got up from the table. Taking my hand, he led me outside to where his car was parked.

As we pulled up outside Aunt Lillian's house, sadness overwhelmed me. I missed Bev as it was my first time in Massachusetts without her and it didn't feel right. Aunt Lillian was enjoying a cup of tea on the porch. "My beautiful Hannah, is that you?" She called out and I ran into her arms. "It's wonderful to see you. Come inside. I'll make some tea." I introduced Alex to her. She had a talent for understanding people's true essence, and I knew she could see his extraordinary qualities.

We talked and laughed for quite a while before she asked me about Bev. "Aunt Lillian, our friendship wasn't as strong as I thought it would be, and so we went our separate ways." She looked at me astonished.

"I can see you don't want to tell the details, so Bev must have done something very hurtful. You had a beautiful friendship and I hope you find your way back to each other one day," Trying to change the subject, I mentioned the upcoming visit to Harvard. Aunt Lillian's eyes filled with tears as she expressed how proud she was of me.

After almost three hours at Aunt Lillian's, I mentioned that we had to leave because of our other plans for the day. Aunt Lillian said she appreciated our visit and told Alex to take good care of me, calling me "one in a million." Alex reassured her and kissed my forehead. Saying goodbye to Aunt Lillian felt surreal. I didn't know if I would ever come back to Massachusetts. It felt like the end of one of the most precious chapters in my life. I walked into my cozy lavender room and sat on the bed, wanting to take everything in and remember it forever. Walking to the window, I looked out at the ocean one last time from my room in Aunt Lillian's house. Tears fell from my eyes as I remembered all the good times I had spent in that room. It will always hold a special place in my heart.

After saying goodbye to Aunt Lillian, I took Alex to the beach. Once again, I found myself doing what I always did – burying my toes in the wet sand, allowing the salt water to caress my feet, and taking in the ocean's fragrance, each unique wave, and the melodious sound of the water. I was finally at my happy place. Taking Alex's hand in mine, I whispered, "Come share in my happiness, my love." It was a perfect moment and I would treasure it forever.

We spent the rest of the day walking through the botanical garden, where Alex surprised me with a picnic he had planned. He had all my favorite food and snacks prepared, even the gummy candy I loved so much. Time flew by as we laughed and chatted, but for me, it felt like time was standing still, just for us. Afterward, we headed off to the carnival where we went on almost all the rides. The adventurous side of Alex was in overdrive. He loved it. He even won me a huge stuffed penguin, which I named Henry. It was a memorable day indeed. "So, have you applied to any colleges yet?" I asked as I stuffed some cotton candy in my mouth.

"No, I'm still weighing all my options, but let's not talk about that now. Come along!" He took my hand and headed toward the rollercoaster. As I heard the terrified screams, my nerves became more and more frazzled. Alex took my face in his hands and reassured me. "Don't be afraid. I'll hold your hand the whole time. This is an amazing experience, Hannah. You don't want to miss it." Just the thought of going on the rollercoaster made me sick to my stomach, but I'd do anything for Alex, so I got on the ride and closed my eyes as I clung to his hand for dear life.

Chapter 17

We arrived at the guesthouse just after midnight, both feeling exhausted. "Thank you for an amazing day, Alex," I said while placing a kiss on his cheek. All I wanted to do was curl up in bed and fall asleep in my boyfriend's arms.

"You're most welcome, Hannah. Let's take a bath," he suggested while pouring some bath salt into the bathtub. Knowing that our time together would be limited due to Harvard weekend, final exams, prom, and graduation preparations, I pushed through my fatigue and enjoyed a relaxing bath with Alex. Ending the day in my boyfriend's arms, sharing a warm bath scented with jasmine, brought me a sense of complete satisfaction. "I think this is it, Hannah. I know fairy tales don't always come true, but I believe we're the exception."

"I believe that too. Like I said before, it will always be you." I said and turned to face him. We made love that night as if Armageddon was upon us. It was unlike anything I ever experienced before. Our bodies moved as one; each touch sent electricity through my body. As I looked into his eyes, I knew I was right where I belonged.

When I opened my eyes the next morning, I didn't want to get up – I didn't want the weekend to be over. So, instead, I just moved my body closer to Alex's and rested my head on his chest. The sound of his heart beating was like a beautiful love song. How was it possible to love him so much? He had my heart and I didn't mind at all. "Good morning, my beautiful Hannah." His voice made me smile automatically. I couldn't even help it.

"Good morning, boyfriend." I knew we had to get ready for the drive back home, but it was the last thing I wanted to do.

"Would you like to go to the beach again before we head back home?" He knew me so well. I nodded and reluctantly got up. At least I could spend some time at my favorite place before we had to go back home. I searched through my suitcase for something to wear before heading of to the bathroom. When I finished, Alex had already gathered all our things. "I'm starving. Let's get some breakfast before I start nibbling on you," He teased and kissed me. While he loaded our luggage in the car, I checked us out at reception.

We decided to buy some breakfast food at the supermarket and have a picnic on the beach. After I ate, I walked toward the ocean to feel the cool water on my skin once more. I was staring at the endless water in front of me when Alex came from behind and lifted me over his shoulder. He ran into the ocean and let me fall into the water. We splashed each other till we were both soaking wet. It was so much fun. "We should probably hit the road, Babe," Alex said panting. He took my hand as we walked toward the car. I played my playlist while we drove and sang along to every song. Every so often, Alex looked at me amused, but I kept at it.

Before long, we were back in Boston and I felt so sad that I wouldn't be spending every moment with Alex anymore. On the contrary, we'd see each other much less. As he pulled up in my driveway, I had to fight back tears. "Thank you for a magical weekend, Alex. I'll never forget it." He carried my luggage inside where he also greeted my mom and exchanged pleasantries, before he turned to me and kissed my forehead.

"Good night, my Hannah. I'll come pick you up in the morning." As soon as he closed the door behind him, my mom bombarded me with questions. I made us some coffee and told her all about the weekend. Well, only the appropriate parts.

"Mom, I'm very tired, is it okay if I take a shower and get in bed?" I asked while I suppressed a yawn. I could tell my mom still wanted to talk more, but she agreed.

"No problem Honey. We can talk tomorrow. We still have to make arrangements for your visit to Harvard this coming weekend." I nodded and headed to my bedroom. It felt depressing laying in my bed alone. I wanted to be in Alex's arms. Reaching for my phone to send him a text, I got one from him. *I miss you in my arms. Sweet dreams, Babe.* I fell asleep with a smile on my face that night.

The next few days went by super fast as I juggled my time between Alex, homework, and preparing for my interview with the Dean of Harvard during the weekend visit. The night before I had to leave for Harvard, I went to Alex's. It would be the first weekend we'd spent apart since we started dating. "Why didn't you call? I could've picked you up." Alex asked when he opened his front door.

"Hello to you too, boyfriend." I kissed him like we were apart for a long time. He picked me up in his arms and went into his bedroom.

"You don't play fair, Hannah," he said while undressing me. I smiled and started undressing him too. He pushed me onto the bed and got on top of me, kissing me all over. I wanted him inside of me, but he took his time teasing me, kissing and caressing my body. I pulled him up, looked into his eyes, and said urgently, "I want you. Now." He entered me, rapidly thrusting in and out of me to the point I could feel my whole body trembling with pleasure. I groaned loudly and clung to his biceps as I climaxed.

"That was fun," Alex teased as we laid naked, side by side on his bed. My body felt too weak to get up, so I turned to face him and caressed his cheek with my hand.

"Want to watch a movie?" I asked, still trying to catch my breath. He nodded and got dressed. Handing me my clothes, he gestured for me to get up. He ordered us some pizza and I picked out a sappy romance movie for us to watch. As he laid with his head in my lap, I caressed his hair. It felt so nice being so intimate with him.

"So, you still haven't told me your plans for after graduation. What colleges did you apply to?" I asked. He turned his gaze to me, his eyes full of excitement.

"I'm not going to college. I want to travel around the world. And you're coming with me." I was stunned, absolutely speechless.

"Alex, I'm going to Harvard. You know I have my heart set on that... How can we have a relationship when you travel around the world? When would we see each other?" For a moment there were complete silence between us.

"Hannah, I had to stay in one place my whole life. I want to see the world, explore and experience everything this life have to offer. Don't you want that?" He sat up straight and held my face in both his hands. "Say you want that too. Please." Tears fell from my eyes as I realized that the worst was happening. We were ending.

"Harvard is my dream, Alex," I couldn't look at him. I couldn't believe that I was losing him again. "Does this mean that.... are we..." Alex took me into his arms and held me close. So close, I could feel his heart beating.

"We still have time. Let's make the most of it. We'll go to prom together and spend every possible moment with each other. Let's just do that and not say anything else." He said, still holding me.

We watched the rest of the movie in silence while we both knew the unspoken truth – that as soon as high school was over, so were we.

That night, as I was lying in my bed, Alex's words kept echoing in my mind. How could life be so cruel to give me such great love and then take it away, just like that? And here I believed true love conquered all.

I unlocked my phone and listened to love songs until I fell asleep. The sound of Alex's voice woke me the next morning, and for a moment, I thought I was dreaming, but then he opened the door to my room and announced: "Look out, Harvard, she's coming!" I couldn't help but laugh at his nerdy announcement. "Get up, Beautiful. I arranged with your mom and I'll be driving you."

"That's great!" I said, getting up. "Give me a few minutes to get ready." I tried to sound excited, even though I was still devastated. As I was getting ready, I heard Alex and my mom talking. I couldn't hear what they said, but I knew Alex wouldn't tell her any personal details of our relationship. I examined myself in the mirror before I picked up my luggage and left my room.

"You look beautiful, Honey. Harvard is so lucky." My mom was super proud, and she made sure I knew it. The aroma of fresh coffee and pancakes was hanging in the air. Alex noticed me looking at it and pointed to a plastic container and travel cup, saying, "You'll have to eat breakfast on the go, Babe." I kissed my mom goodbye and headed to Alex's car, feeling nervous about how we were going to avoid the topic neither of us wanted to acknowledge.

Luckily, the drive to Harvard wasn't too long. We talked about what we would wear to the senior prom. We arranged study sessions for our final exams and he told me that his mom was pregnant again. There were no awkward silence moments between us. As he pulled up at the university, I gasped at the masses of students walking around the vast campus. "Don't feel overwhelmed, Hannah. You've got this. Come along." He winked at me as he got out of the car and unloaded my luggage. I admired the confidence Alex was showing while he made his way through the students, and I wondered whether I would ever reach that level of confidence. He walked me to my dorm room, where I'd be staying for the weekend. "I'll be back to pick you up on Sunday, okay? Try to have fun, Babe."

I hesitated. "Alex, I don't want to stay. I want to be with you." My heart was racing and I couldn't catch my breath. He held me and whispered in my ear.

"This is where you belong, Hannah. This is your dream." I held on to him a few moments longer before I let go. He kissed my hand and then walked away. It took every ounce of strength in me to not run after him. I was so lost in my emotions that I didn't hear the door open behind me.

"Hi. You must be Hannah." Startled, I turned around to see a girl with curly blonde hair, dressed in a bright pink tracksuit and sneakers, grinning at me. "I'm Tessa," she continued.

"Pleased to meet you," I said while holding out my hand, but she hugged me instead. She was my roommate for the weekend, and she was also just what I needed: a hefty dose of happy-go-lucky.

"A bunch of us newbies are going to a cafe on campus for milkshakes. Come on." I didn't feel like being around a bunch of strangers and making small talk, but Tessa refused to leave me alone. So, I surrendered and went along. The cafe had an antique vibe to it and I liked it. I could picture myself sitting there with my books, studying for a test. We approached a table where two girls and three boys were sipping on milkshakes. "Guys, this here is Hannah. Hannah, this is the guys." I smiled at them, feeling self-conscious.

"Have a seat, Hannah. "I'm Eric," he said, introducing himself. He had dark brown hair and green eyes, and his skin had a tanned light brown complexion. I smiled and grabbed a seat. The rest of the gang also introduced themselves. They were Danny, Jason, Amelia and Emily. I could tell that Emily wasn't too happy to meet me, but I focused on the rest instead. We talked about our expectations for the weekend and what we wanted to study.

I had so much fun that I didn't even notice the time until Jason suggested that we should call it a night. Me, Jason and Eric went to our respective rooms, while the rest decided to stay at the café a bit longer. As soon as I got in my room, I changed into my pajamas and called Alex. We talked for about ten minutes before we hung up. I was so tired, when my head hit the pillow, I was asleep.

I woke up the next morning, both excited and still tired. Tessa wasn't in her bed and I didn't hear her come in the night before. I got up and got ready for the day. We were all supposed to meet at the café in an hour for a tour of the campus. Thereafter, we would have individual interviews with the Dean. After I showered and got dressed, I went to the café and bought myself a cappuccino. James and Eric were there, also enjoying some coffee. I waved at them and walked outside, where I wanted to enjoy my coffee, while calling Alex. As I made my way outside, I bumped into Tessa. She was wearing a pair of loose jeans and a yellow top with red polka dots on it, making it difficult not to notice her. "Good morning, Hannah Banana!" She said teasingly. I chuckled as I greeted her. I admired the way she was true to herself. It was no surprise when she told me she wanted to major in acting. I was sure she'd be a brilliant actress one day.

A tall brunette girl approached us. Her beauty was astonishing and left me feeling intimated. "Hi, ladies. I'm Kate and I'll be your guide today. Are the others inside?" Her voice was as beautiful as she was.

Tessa spoke before I had the chance. Agitated, she said: "Yes, Kate." Taken aback, I shifted my attention to Tessa as a visibly upset Kate made her way into the café. "She's my pain-in-the-ass cousin," Tessa explained. I just nodded, not asking questions. "Give me that coffee. I'm sure I need it more than you." I erupted in laughter and handed her the cappuccino.

"I like you, Tess." She smiled at me sweetly. Just then, Kate and the two boys joined us. Kate cleared her throat.

"The others will meet us a bit later. So, the tour will be about an hour long. Once we finish, I'll assign each of you a specific time slot for your interview with the Dean. In the meantime, you are welcome to attend classes, just to get the feel or you could entertain yourself however you wish."

I was left speechless, in complete awe of everything Harvard offered. It was so much better than what I had read. There were so many students sitting on the grass, having breakfast and talking. Some of them were reading under a tree, while others were making out. I just loved every part of that campus and couldn't wait to be part of it. After the tour, everyone went their separate ways. My interview with the Dean was in two hours, so I called Alex. I had just hung up when Eric and Tessa approached me. Eric was carrying a brown paper bag and two coffees. "We brought breakfast!" Tessa announced. Eric laughed and shook his head.

"You bullied me to buy breakfast." Tessa elbowed him in his rib and looked at me, amused.

"Come, Hannah. Let's sit on the grass like proper students." I enjoyed getting to know Tessa and Eric better, and we made plans to meet up later that night again. Soon it was time for my interview. Tessa threw her arms around me. "You'll do great, Hannah Banana!"

Eric looked at me, confused, "Banana? Seriously?" I just shrugged, giggling.

"See you guys later!"

Chapter 18

I left the Dean's office feeling great and all I wanted to do, was celebrate with my boyfriend. I pulled my phone out and texted him: *"Hi Babe. The interview went great. Wish I could celebrate with you right now. Missing you."*

I was walking toward my dorm room, deep in thought, when the sound of Eric's voice pulled me back to reality. "Hannah! How was the interview?" I could tell he was nervous, so I tried to calm him.

"Don't stress. The Dean is friendly. I promise you have nothing to worry about. Okay?" He looked at me and I swore his eyes were a shade of green I'd never seen before. He told me he was the first one in his family to go to college, so there was a lot of pressure on him. I felt a strong sense of admiration towards him. It was so weird, it was like we'd been friends for a long time. As he walked to the Dean's office, I said a silent prayer for him.

I wanted to take a nap while Eric and Tessa finished their interviews, but I couldn't sleep. My mind was racing with thoughts of me and Alex. I didn't want to break up with him, I didn't want to relive the heartache again and I didn't want to live a life without him in it, but I knew in my bones that no matter what happened, our love would always have a special place in both our hearts. And with that thought, I drifted into a peaceful sleep.

When Tessa woke me up, it was already dark out. "I have a surprise for you!" She said and pointed to the door where Alex was standing with a bouquet of pink roses in his hands. I jumped to my feet and ran into his arms.

"I am so happy you came," I said, as tears of joy welled up in my eyes.

"Of course I did, Hannah. We have to celebrate. What do you want to do?" I wanted to go home with him, but Tessa and the others had already made plans for us to go for drinks and dancing later that night.

Tessa quickly declared, "We're all going out tonight, including you, Alex." Alex's disappointment showed, but he nodded and looked at me. "That's all I want – to be with my Hannah." I smiled, but I couldn't help resenting him a little. He said he wanted to be with me, yet he chose to travel around the world, ending our relationship. Of course, I couldn't expect him to give up his dream for me when I wasn't willing to do the same. I pushed my conflicted feelings aside to enjoy the night with my boyfriend and new friends.

The next morning, I shifted a few times in the seat of the car to find a comfortable position. "This is going to be a long drive," I said, feeling irritated. My body was sore from all the dancing the night before and my head was pounding.

"I'll do my best to drive safely and quickly, Babe, but it's important for you to know your limit with liquor." I couldn't tell whether he was mad or disappointed. Either way, it made me feel even worse.

When we said goodbye to Tessa and the others earlier that morning, Alex seemed a little preoccupied, but I didn't want to ask him about it. Partly because I suspected it was due to my alcohol intake the previous night. Despite the massive hangover and body ache I was suffering from, it was a great weekend. I was sure that Harvard was where I belonged. I turned the radio on to break the silence between us and closed my eyes.

"Hannah! Are you seriously going to sleep while I'm driving? I was also up late last night." It took me a moment to realize that Alex was yelling at me. I knew that something else was upsetting him, and I wanted to understand it.

"What's bothering you, Alex?" I asked calmly while struggling to tie my hair in a ponytail. "Hannah, did you notice how Eric was looking at you and how he danced only with you? I hate the thought of you with another guy. It's killing me." Tears were falling from his eyes, and my heart shattered. That was the first time I saw him cry.

"Alex, please pull over," I asked, my voice cracking. As soon as the car stopped moving, I kissed him like it would be the last time. I didn't want to stop. "I don't want anyone else, Alex. My heart belongs to you." I climbed onto his lap and laid my head on his chest while he held me tight. We sat like that for quite some time before we continued driving. Being with him while knowing we were going to end eventually, was excruciating. And I knew he felt the same.

"Will I see you tonight? He asked hopefully. I couldn't say no, even though I just wanted to soak in a warm bubble bath and enjoy a good night's sleep.

"Only if you'll make us some pasta." I was starving and he made the best pasta I'd ever tasted. "Let me just check in with my Mom first okay?" He nodded kissed my forehead before carrying my luggage into the house. He greeted my mom and headed home.

"Hannah, Honey, tell my everything" I filled my mom in on everything. I told her about my new friends, the café, the campus, the trees and the interview with the Dean. "Honey, I'm so excited for you, but... " She stared at the floor.

""What's wrong mom?" I asked anxiously, expecting the worst.

She inhaled deeply. "Well, Dave... he..." I held my hand up and interrupted her abruptly.

"Mom, you know he is already dead to me. I mourned him months ago." She still didn't make eye contact with me.

"Honey, the funeral is..." I felt agitated and interrupted her again.

"Mom, please! He's been dead to me for months now. I'm not going to any funeral." I stormed off to my room and texted Alex, asking him to pick me up. I threw on some fresh clothes without showering. I wanted to get out of the house as quickly as I could. "Mom, I'm off to Alex's okay?" I announced as I walked toward the front door.

"Hannah, please don't be mad. I respect your decision, but as your mom it was my obligation to tell you what happened and lay all the options on the table." I couldn't blame my mom for having a beautiful heart, so I apologized and embraced her. "Don't come home too late, okay?" I nodded and headed outside where Alex was already waiting in his car.

We studied together for a few hours and then we just talked and laughed while we ate some pasta. He handed me a little black box, saying, "This is something to commemorate all the amazing times we shared." In the box was a necklace with a seashell shaped pendant. Engraved on the back of the pendant were the words "H & A - For Always."

"Alex, this is precious. I'll treasure it forever." I thanked him with a long and passionate kiss.

"Lets just be with each other tonight, no sex. I want you close to me." Every day, he just got more amazing. I loved him to my very core. How was I supposed to get over him, ever?

I sat on his lap, rested my head on his shoulder, and whispered, "Alex, what we share is a great love. Nothing and no one will ever compare." He said nothing, but his silence spoke volumes.

The days went by; it was like a blur. Soon, finals were over, and the senior prom was upon us. My mom took me shopping. We had loads of fun, but I missed Bev so much. I wished she hadn't broken our friendship. Mom interrupted my thoughts when she presented me with a gorgeous strapless black dress with tiny rhinestones across the chest. It was plain but gracefully refined.

"Mom, I love it!" And just like that, I had my dress for prom. Afterward, we went to the hairdresser and beautician. I tried to protest, but she insisted, so I just went along with it. When we got home, I examined myself in the full-length mirror in my mom's room, and I was more satisfied than I expected to be with what I saw. Just then, Alex knocked on the front door.

"Hannah, don't come out yet!" my mom yelled from inside. She wanted to capture each moment on camera. When she called me, and I saw Alex in his black tuxedo, my knees got so weak I had to stand still for a moment.

"Hannah, you look exquisite." Alex said while handing me a corsage with white lilies on.

"You're not too bad yourself." I said, kissing him on the cheek. I glanced over at my mom who was wiping tears from her eyes. "Mom, are you okay?" I asked teasingly. She just nodded and continued taking pictures. The reality suddenly hit me. We were going to our senior prom. It was a bitter-sweet moment. We - Alex and me, would soon be just a memory. "Can we please go now mom?" She let out a sigh and agreed.

"Enjoy it you guys. It only comes around once." Much like the love me and Alex shared, I thought to myself.

Soon, we arrived at prom. Everything and everyone were so beautiful. There was a magical atmosphere hanging in the air, like anything was possible. As we slow danced, I held onto Alex like I never wanted to let go. We both knew that the end was drawing near, but we didn't talk about it. We only made the most of each moment we had together. When prom was over, we went to Alex's house and he led me to his bedroom, which he turned into what looked like a romantic scene out of a movie. The room was filled with rose petals and candles. On a tray was a bottle champagne and two glasses. It was obvious that he put in a lot to make the evening special - and it was. The whole experience was surreal – the way we kissed, made love and laid tangled in each other afterwards. The whole night was like a fairytale and I never felt more special. "I know you have to go home, but I really don't want to let you go." I knew his words had a much deeper meaning, so I didn't say anything. I just held him a bit tighter.

The next morning , I was having breakfast, when my mom came running into the kitchen, yelling: "It's here! It's the big envelope!" When I saw the envelope in my mom's hands, I knew that I got in to Harvard. I squealed and jumped into her arms. "I'm so proud of you, Honey!" I tore open the envelope and scanned through the letter quickly. When I saw the word "accepted," I immediately called Alex and told him. I hung up and hugged Mom once more. "All that's left now is Graduation and my baby girl will be out of the house." Mom started crying.

"Not again, Mom." I said, wiping her tears away. She smiled and held my face in her hands.

"You are the very best part of me, Hannah. I love you. Now, finish your breakfast please." She left the kitchen and I perused the letter and brochures carefully. Graduation was in three days and then high school would officially be over.

I received a text from Alex saying that he was outside and needed to talk to me. I immediately headed outside and joined him in his car. "Hannah, I have to tell you something." He took my hand in his and let out a sigh. I inhaled deeply in anticipation. "I'll be leaving for Spain after Graduation. I'll be there for about two weeks before I begin my traveling." I remained silent for quite a while. "Hannah? Are you going to say something?" He looked so worried that I forced myself to speak.

"There's nothing to say, Alex. We both knew this moment was inevitable. Now it's here." I fought back my tears with all my strength. "I think we should end it now. Let's not fall any deeper." He didn't say anything. He just took me in his arms and held me. I could feel him crying and my tears started falling too. We stayed like that – in each other's arms for a long time. I didn't want to let go. When we finally slowly pulled away from each other, I gently grazed his cheek with my hand and whispered: "You will forever be my always." He kissed me one last time.

"Always - my Hannah." I got out of the car and without looking back, I went inside the house, where I broke down in tears. I cried until my eyes were sore. "Hannah? What's wrong?" Mom had just woken up from her nap and found me on the floor of the lounge. I told her everything while she sat beside me, caressing my hair.

I spent the next few days packing and preparing for college, trying to keep my mind of Alex. I went shopping for new clothes and even got a hair cut, but nothing worked. I kept thinking about him, I smelled him, I even dreamed of him. I missed him so intensely. I was constantly at war with myself to stay away from him. It was exhausting.

Graduation day arrived and It would be the first time I'd see Alex since we broke up. I was beyond nervous. The ceremony was beautiful and the valedictorian's speech was very moving. After everyone received their diplomas, we had celebratory drinks on the football field – another tradition. I was standing alone, sipping on champagne, when I saw Bev approaching me. I didn't have enough energy to face her, so I turned and walked away. "Hannah!" I heard Elijah calling, but I didn't turn around. I walked faster, straight home. Suddenly a car pulled up beside me. It was Alex. He got out, saying nothing, he took me in his arms and kissed me, like he couldn't breathe without me. I didn't want the kiss to end. He picked me up and I wrapped my legs around his waist. I ran my fingers through his hair and savored every detail of the kiss. When we stopped to catch our breath, he gently put me down as we looked into each other's eyes. He whispered: "Always." I turned and walked away with heavy feet, feeling devastated. It was really over.

Chapter 19

The first month of college was hectic. It was a huge adjustment getting used to college life. I attended loads of classes, walked around on campus whenever I could and, hung out with my friends. I missed my mom and my own room though, not to mention Alex. I haven't heard from him since Graduation, but I kept track of his movements on social media.

I was setting up a schedule for the next week's classes, when I began to feel faint and nauseous. I tried to stand up of the bed, but I got a blinding pain in my lower stomach. Reaching for my phone to call Tessa, Eric knocked on the door. "Come in!" I yelled. He rushed to my side when he saw me leaning on the table, moaning from the pain.

"Hannah! What's wrong?" His eyes were wide and I could hear the fear clearly in his voice. I told him how I was feeling and he picked me up in his arms. "I'm taking you to the emergency room. You look very ill." I wanted to protest, but everything suddenly went dark. When I opened my eyes again, we were in the hospital and medical personnel surrounded me. I was in and out of consciousness. The only thing I was fully aware of was the excruciating pain in my stomach. I heard the doctor calling my name, but I couldn't speak. I felt extremely weak. All I wanted was my mom.

"Hannah?" An unfamiliar voice called. I struggled to open my eyes. "Hi there Hannah. I'm Doctor Reed. You're at the Beck Memorial Hospital. How are you feeling?" I cleared my throat before I tried to speak.

"I feel confused and very sore. What happened Doctor? He scratched his head and I could tell it wasn't good news. I expected him to say that I had the kidney disease Dave suffered from, but I wasn't prepared for what he actually said.

"Hannah, you had a miscarriage. I'm so sorry." I was stunned. How was that even possible.

"How... when...I don't understand." I had to fight hard to keep my tears at bay.

"You were about nine weeks pregnant. Hannah, I'll send a counselor to see you. Once again, I'm very sorry." He walked out of the room, leaving me in total disbelief. I reached for my phone and texted Alex, asking him to come see me. Eric entered the room and rushed to hug me.

"Are you okay? You gave me a huge fright." I didn't know why, but it felt like I've known him my whole life and I trusted him completely. "You can tell me, Hannah." He reassured me.

Without making eye contact, I told him what happened, while tears streamed down my face. He consoled me, holding me in his arm and telling me that everything would be okay. "Eric, I don't even know how I should feel. Should I be happy? Sad? Relieved ?" He said nothing and just held me a little tighter. I cried myself to sleep in his arms.

When I opened my eyes again, Tessa and Eric were sitting next to my bed, both drinking coffee. "How are you feeling, Banana?" Tessa asked with a worried face. I haven't seen that side of her yet. She was always so happy.

"I'm good, Tessa. Please don't worry about me." I said, trying to sound nonchalant. She nodded, but I could see she didn't believe me. Just then, Alex walked into the room, but he wasn't alone. Camila, his fling from the summer before, was with him. I felt a sting of jealousy as I studied her perfect features.

"Hannah, are you okay?" I wanted to yell at him to leave. How could he have already moved on while my heart still longed for him? Eric got up and announced that they should leave and give me and Alex some privacy. He and Tessa left the room, but Camila stayed. She wrapped her arm around Alex like she was marking her territory. I decided right there and then that I wouldn't tell him about the pregnancy or miscarriage.

"Alex, I'm sorry that you had to come all this way. I sent you a text while I was under the influence of strong pain medication. I'm fine. You can go," I snapped, but he knew me too well. He looked at me like he could see into my soul, like he could see the love I still had for him in my heart. For a few heartbeats, it was just me and him, while the rest of the world stood still.

Camilla cleared her throat and Alex said, "Hannah, I know you're lying, but it's fine. We'll be staying at the Blossom Hotel for the night. Call me when you're ready to talk, okay?" I nodded and my heart broke as they walked out together. I promised myself then that I would never contact Alex again.

As I was recovering, Tessa had to go home due to a family emergency and Eric stepped in to take care of me. He cheered me up and encouraged me to stay positive. I trusted him with my secret and he was the only one who knew about it. The more time we spent together, the more I found myself liking him. He had a humble and comforting presence that put me at ease. Although I was physically healed, emotionally, I still needed some mending and I knew exactly what to do. "Eric, will you please take me to the beach?"

He looked at me confused. "You know it's cold outside, right?"

Nodding, I replied : "I need some medicine for this broken heart of mine. It's time for me to go to my happy place." He reluctantly agreed to take me.

We arrived at the beach just as the sun was setting. I took off my shoes and rolled up my jeans as I walked toward the ocean, inviting Eric to join me. Sitting on the sand, we were both mesmerized by the beauty of the sunset over the ocean, and I could feel my mood lifting.

"Wow, Hannah, I see what you mean. This is food for the soul," Eric said, sounding surprised. I asked him if this was his first time seeing a sunset on the beach, and he admitted that it wasn't, but he had never appreciated it like that before. He thanked me for letting him experience it with me. As I turned to look at him, our eyes met, and he suddenly kissed me. "Is this okay?" he asked as he pulled away slowly.

"Don't stop," I said, my voice hoarse. He kissed me again, and it felt so good. I didn't think I could ever enjoy kissing another boy after Alex, but I did. I truly did.

"Hannah, I like you a lot, but I don't want to be a rebound and get my heart broken. One thing you have to know about me is, when I commit to something, I'm all in. So, let's just take things slow okay?" His powerful words left me weak. I nodded my head with much effort. What he said made sense, but I was sure that he wouldn't be a rebound. He was the complete opposite of Alex and Elijah too, for that matter. He was dependable and predictable, but in a good way. He was loving, caring, and loyal, but his maturity was what attracted me the most. The fact that he was super hot was just a major bonus.

"I understand, Eric. Just know that you won't be a rebound. You mean too much to me." I kissed his cheek and then turned my gaze back to the ocean and enjoyed every bit of serenity it offered for as long as I could.

When we arrived back in my dorm room, I suggested that we watch a movie, but he declined, saying that he was tired and needed some sleep, but I had a suspicion that he was avoiding being alone with me. So, I watched a movie all by myself for the first time since I could remember. It was always me and Bev, me and Elijah or me and Alex. It felt weird at first, but after a while, it was quite nice. Maybe I needed to be by myself for a bit, I thought to myself. I could focus on my studies without any distractions and have time for some much needed self care. I always wanted to do yoga and it was the perfect time to learn. I cleared my mind and turned my attention back to the movie while snuggling under the blanket.

My alarm woke me at 8am the next morning. I had class in an hour, but I still felt tired. Getting up, I felt light headed and was about to text Eric to bring some breakfast when someone knocked on the door. As fate would have it, it was Eric with coffee and bagels. "Good morning. You're an angel. Thanks so much," I said in one breath before digging into a bagel.

"Good morning, Hannah," Eric said between chuckles. "I'm happy to see your appetite is back. Well, if you don't need anything else, I'm off to class." I grabbed his hand and pulled him close. For a moment, I contemplated kissing him, but I hugged him instead.

"Thank you, Eric. For everything." I whispered. He nodded with a smile and headed out the door. I finished my breakfast and made my way to the bathroom to shower and get dressed for the day's classes. I signed up for two additional courses in addition to my usual classes, so I had a busy semester ahead.

Tessa was supposed to return later that day and I was super excited to see her again. Her presence made such a huge difference in a room. She exerted happiness and positivity on another level, and I loved how I could completely be myself around her. She and Eric were my lifeline at college. I could depend on them.

As time passed, I found myself becoming more and more attracted to Eric. Even Tessa noticed. I wanted to ask him out, but my fear of rejection held me back. Instead, I kept arranging group outings for the three of us, just so I could spend time with him, even if it wasn't just the two of us. Tessa did her best to encourage me to make a move, but I remained hesitant.

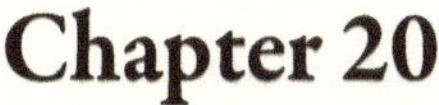

Chapter 20

I made it through my first and second years of college. Tessa was my best friend, and Eric was my boyfriend. We had only been together for a year, and life was perfect, well, almost. Juggling a friendship, a relationship, good grades, and my relationship with my mom was much more challenging than I had anticipated. I felt stressed most of the time, which led to frequent arguments with the most important people in my life. Luckily, they understood the pressure I was under and supported me.

"Do you want to go out with me tonight?" Eric asked as he put his arm around my waist. We were walking to the café to get some coffee before class.

"That would be nice, but I need to study for a test tomorrow. I'm sorry," I said, genuinely bummed.

"You can come over for a quick coffee and a good night kiss before you go to bed tonight," I said, putting my hand in the back pocket of his jeans.

"Marking your territory, are you?" he asked teasingly, and I chuckled. "Well, I like it," he said and kissed me on my forehead.

I was so focused in my studies that I didn't even hear Tessa calling my name until she tapped me on the shoulder. "Hannah, it's almost 2am. You need to get some sleep."

Confused, I asked: "Had Eric been here?" I couldn't believe that time flew by so fast.

Tessa shook her head. "He wasn't here. Was he supposed to come?"

I immediately checked my phone, but there were no messages or missed calls from him. "Well, he was, but something probably came up." I said, trying to act like it didn't bother me, but really, anxiousness was consuming me. After our conversation, I couldn't sleep. My mind was in overdrive. I kept creating the worst scenarios where Eric cheated on me. After all, if there was anything I had learned from my previous relationships, it was that nothing good lasted forever.

I laid awake all night and when my alarm went of, I got up quietly as not to wake Tessa and went to the bathroom. When I returned, Eric was waiting in front of the door.

"I'm so sorry, Hannah...." He began to explain, but I interrupted him.

"It doesn't matter. You can keep on doing whatever and whomever you were doing last night. I'm done wasting my time." I snapped. His eyes widened and he opened his mouth to speak again, but I pushed him aside and entered the room.

"Hannah! I fell asleep!" His words were like a slap across my face. "But it's good to know what you think of me." He said as he walked away before I could reply.

Tessa was awake and looked at me with a composed expression. "Dude, how could you think he would cheat on you? That guy is so deeply in love with you. Are you blind?" I didn't know how to answer her, so I just picked up my phone and headed to class.

I completed the test effortlessly and went to the café for coffee afterward, where I ran into Eric.

"Eric. I'm so sorry. I don't know what's wrong with me. Please forgive me." I pleaded. He looked at me lovingly, which somehow made me feel worse.

"Hannah, I know you've been hurt, and I understand that you have trust issues because of that. It's not your fault. I love you, but for us to move forward together, I need you to seek closure from your past." When he spoke those words, I realized what I had to do. I had to confront Elijah and forgive him. I needed to let go of what he did to me.

"I love you too, and I'll do whatever I need to make us work. If I'm not mistaken, Elijah is studying at Columbia. Do you want to come with me to New York?" I asked, hoping that he would say yes. The idea of exploring the city with him seemed wonderful, but he declined, leaving me disappointed.

"No, Hannah. This is something you have to do on your own," he said, taking a sip of his coffee. "I am completely committed to you, to us. If you're willing to work through your past and have confidence in me, I think our love can last forever."

I wanted that, I needed that. When looked into his eyes, I could see my future. I met his family in Chicago during Thanksgiving and got their approval. His mom was, much like mine, a kind-hearted woman. She made me feel at ease and spoiled me rotten with home baked goods. His dad, on the other hand, was a man of few words. He only spoke when necessary, but I could tell that he liked me when he told me about the days when he would go fishing with Eric and his older brother, Lucas. He asked me whether I liked fishing too and I told a little white lie, to win over his favor. Unfortunately, Lucas was in Turkey on business when we visited so I didn't get to meet him. Nonetheless, I had a wonderful time with the Clark family.

We were planning to visit my mom in a month when classes dialed down. I've told her all about Eric over the phone and she was already crazy about him, so meeting him would just be a formality. Of course, Tessa invited herself along, but I didn't mind it at all. She sprinkled her "happy dust" everywhere she went and we could all use loads of it.

Eric was lying on my bed while I was packing for New York. I had booked myself into a hotel for two nights , because I wanted to explore a bit of the city while I was there. "I really wish you'd come with me, Eric." I hinted, but he shook his head.

"No, Sweets. I told you, you need to do this alone. And when you return, I'll be waiting for you here, with a big surprise." He had a wide grin on his face, which excited me.

"I really want to know what it is, but I know you well enough to not even bother asking." I said while I packed the last of my clothes.

He smiled and pulled me on top of him. "I'll miss you."

I kissed him and then whispered in his ear: "How about one for the road?" He smiled mischievously, got up, and locked the door. He picked me up and sat me down on the desk. He tried to take my top off. Struggling, he yelled: "so many buttons!" I chuckled, but then he ripped open my top, which instantly turned me on. He was the perfect gentleman, but in the bedroom, he was a complete bad boy. I loved it. He thrust in and out of me, making me groan in overwhelming pleasure. Every sense of my being was heightened with desire. Touching his hot, naked body was enough to send me over the edge. He knew exactly how to please me, what moves to make, and what to touch. The whole experience was excessive and I loved every minute of it. I moaned so loudly as I climaxed that he had to cover my mouth with his hand.

"Wow!" I said as I grasped for air. "How can each time be better than the time before?"

He chuckled, also out of breath, and kissed me on my hand. "It's because I love you more each day." I hugged him tightly and stayed like that for a few moments.

On the flight to New York, I imagined how it would be seeing Elijah again. I didn't tell him I was coming, partly because I was hoping that I wouldn't be able to find him. I had no idea what I would say to him or how I would act. Somewhere between my conflicted thoughts, I fell asleep and only woke up when the flight attended announced that we were about to land in New York City. The airport was the biggest one I've ever seen. I ordered a cab and enjoyed the sights as we drove to the hotel. I was amazed at the beautiful city and its people. Almost everyone were dressed in labeled clothing. The driver parked in front of The AW Hotel, where I'd be staying. I got out and thanked him as he handed me my luggage.

My room was cozy, with décor of beige and white. The smell of vanilla hung in the air and it had an amazing view of the city. I pulled out my phone to call Eric and saw it was only 4pm. I would have enough time to shower and put on some fresh clothes before heading to Columbia. I called Eric and told him about my plans. Afterward, I went outside and hailed a cab, like a real New Yorker. While we drove, I went on social media, in the hopes of seeing where Elijah was. As luck would have it, he checked into a bar near the campus just half an hour ago. I stepped into the bar, feeling out of place and self conscious. Scanning through the crowded room, a familiar feeling of butterflies fluttering in my stomach started when I saw him. He was much more muscular than I remember. How was it possible that he still had that effect on me after everything he'd done? I was about to turn around, when he yelled my name. "Hannah!" He came running and picked me up in his arms. My knees went weak and I could feel my cheeks heating as I blushed. I wanted to slap myself for allowing him to still effect me like that. "What are you doing here?" His breath smelled like beer, which was about the only thing unattractive about him.

"Hi Elijah. I'm actually here to talk to you." I said, trying not to sound like an blithering idiot I was sure I looked like.

"Well then, let's." He took my hand and led me outside. Twirling me around, he said: "Wow, Hannah. You're still gorgeous. I'm so sorry..." I held my hand up to stop him.

"Elijah, I came here to get closure. Please let me say my peace." He nodded and took a step backwards. "I don't think you can comprehend how much you hurt me when you slept with my best friend. You betrayed my trust and as a result, I'm struggling to trust a man who loves me , like really loves me. He is paying for your mistake, which is not fair." Eric inhaled and was about to speak, but I stopped him again. "I'm not finished." I said abruptly. "For Eric and only for him, I forgive you. I'm officially letting you go. You no longer occupy a place in my heart. The great love we shared, is now just a great tragedy." I let out a sigh of relieve as I envisioned a weight lifting of my shoulders.

"Hannah, I'm sorry for hurting you and for breaking us. Thank you for forgiving me, but, I think you know that out love will always have a place in your heart, as it will in mine." He took my face in both his hands and kissed me. I felt everything I used to feel. It was like nothing had changed, but everything did. I pulled away and grazed his cheek with my hand.

"You're right. You were my first love and you'll always have a place in my heart. Take care of yourself, Elijah." I walked away and officially ended the last chapter of my first love story.

Chapter 21

I called Eric as I entered my hotel room and told him that I saw Elijah and got the closure I sought. He was just as relieved as I was. We talked for a while before we said goodbye. I fell into a peaceful sleep almost immediately.

The next morning, I woke up to the sound of rain falling on the roof. I looked outside the window and saw it was pouring outside. It would be impossible to explore the city in that weather, and I missed Eric so much anyway that I decided to take a flight back later that day. I got up, amended my flight details online, and went to the bathroom to get ready. After I got dressed and packed my things, I ordered a cab.

As I walked out of the hotel building, I looked around the city one last time, and then I saw the Empire State Building and got a powerful urge to go see it. As I got into the cab, I asked the driver to take me there. I was beyond excited as I entered the building with much anticipation. When the elevator door opened to the top of the building, I got out, bracing myself. The view was like nothing I've ever seen before and the rain made it that much more enchanting. I took out my phone, turned around, and took a selfie. Just then, the airline sent me an email informing me they had postponed my flight because of the bad weather. Feeling disappointed, I turned my gaze to the masses of people admiring the view. And then it happened – it was serendipity. There, on top of the Empire State Building, between hundreds of people, was Alex, looking at me. For a moment, time stood still. It was only the two of us on that building. I could hear my heart pounding and felt my body going numb. As he approached me, I got goosebumps. I was in shock. What a sick sense of humour the universe had, I thought to myself.

"Hi, Hannah." I opened my mouth, but no words came out. Instead, my eyes filled with tears. Before I could comprehend what was happening, he took me in his arms and kissed me. It felt like the world was spinning. So many feelings resurfaced all at once. Scenes of moments we shared flashed before my eyes. I pulled away and asked what he was doing. He looked at me with a naughty expression on his face. "I'm sorry Hannah. Let's just blame it on the force of habit. What are you doing here?" He asked, looking down at my luggage.

"Well," I said, knowing that he'd be intrigued, "you wouldn't believe me if I told you."

He smiled and replied, "Sounds like something you can tell me over dinner?" I hesitated for a moment, but then he continued, "Don't worry. I won't kiss you again." I laughed and agreed to have dinner with him. He picked up my luggage and asked where I was headed. When I told him about my flight being delayed, he offered that I could stay with him. "I'll sleep on the couch. There's no need to waste money on a hotel, Hannah. Don't you trust me?" I reluctantly accepted his offer on the condition that there would be no physical contact between us. "For some unexplainable reason, we have a magnetic pull between us. So the more distance is between us, the better it will be." I said bluntly. I could see he was hiding a smile, and I also got the urge to laugh.

The restaurant of the hotel he was staying at was so fancy it made me feel uncomfortable in my jeans and hoodie. "Alex, why didn't you tell me to wear something more formal?"

He looked at me confused and said: "Hannah, you could wear your pajamas and you'd still be the most beautiful woman in the room" He was still such a smooth talker. I perused the menu and ordered the pasta and a glass red wine. I told Alex what the purpose of my visit to New York was and he told me all about his travels. We talked and laughed until the waiter came over to tell us that the restaurant was closing. We polished almost three bottles of red wine and I felt a bit buzzed. As we entered his room, I tripped and Alex caught me. Out faces were so close together that a kiss was inevitable.

"You see? Magnetic," I whispered and he kissed me. He lifted me in his arms and carried me to the bedroom where he laid me on the bed and made love to me like the very first time, passionately and gentle. It felt like no time had passed, like nothing had changed. I laid in his arm, panting.

"Hannah, I still love you." His confession left me astounded. And suddenly, I thought about the last time I saw him. I was in pain, physically and emotionally and he was with Camilla. If we were to try again, we had to do it right, which meant that I had to tell him the truth.

"Alex, I have to tell you something. The reason I was in the hospital was because I had a miscarriage. I was unknowingly pregnant and lost the baby at nine weeks." I didn't look at him. He didn't say anything. After what felt like hours, he silently got dressed and left the room. He'd been gone for two hours when I decided to take a shower and head to the airport. I was busy writing him a note , when he came in. "Really, Hannah? A note? Do I mean so little to you that you kept such a huge secret from me for so long and now you want to leave without saying goodbye?"

His words awoken a rage within me. "I'm sorry, but you had already moved on, remember? You had the audacity to show up at the hospital with Camilla. Can you imagine how I felt?"

He scratched his head vigorously. "It wasn't serious. We were just hanging out." He fell to his knees and cried, "What happened to us, Hannah? It was supposed to always be us."

I sat on the floor beside him and said softly, "You left, Alex. You chose to leave. Are you ready to settle down now and build a future with me?" He stared at the floor, not saying anything, but his answer echoed loudly in the silence. I got up after a while, picked up my luggage and walked away, but when I reached the doorway, I turned around, "Alex, it will always be you. No matter what. No matter the time or distance." And so, I left New York, closing the chapter of my greatest love story.

The whole flight back, I had to fight back tears. I knew that if I allowed myself to cry, I wouldn't be able to stop. I was at war with myself about whether I should tell Eric about my encounter with Alex. The right thing would be honesty, but it just didn't feel worth risking our beautiful relationship. Nothing was going to happen with Alex. We weren't going to get back together and even though we still loved each other and probably always would, I couldn't let an amazing man like Eric slip through my fingers just for the prospective of maybe one day being with Alex again. I had to let go of Alex, but I knew that the bigger part of me didn't want to. I closed my eyes in the hopes of when I opened them again, I would have some clarity.

I woke up just as we were about to land, but I was still as confused as I was before. Looking out the window, I thought about what I had with Alex and what I had with Eric. It couldn't be compared, because it was two completely different loves. As I got off the plane, I realized that I was expecting Alex to change who he was, which wasn't fair. Our timing was just off and no amount of love could fix that. So, it would be Eric. Our timing was perfect and so was our love, and that's why I owed it to him to tell the truth.

I took a cab to campus. I wanted to gather all my strength and emotionally prepare before I confessed the ugly truth to Eric. Tessa wasn't in our room, so I put down my luggage and plunged on the bed. I laid there for a few minutes before heading to the bathroom. I wished that the water could wash away all the bad in my life, all the bad I had done. When I got back in my room, Eric was sitting on my bed. "Why didn't you tell me you were back? I could've picked you up at the airport. Are you okay?" He had a worried expression one his face which made my guilty feelings sky rocket.

"I'm sorry. I just didn't want to bother you." I knew it was a weak excuse, but I couldn't think of anything else to say. Looking at him, I got so mad at myself for betraying him. He didn't deserve that. I didn't want to lose him. I sat next to him, putting his arm around me and just savoured the feeling of being close to him. I laid my head against his and whispered: "I love you." I could feel him smiling and for a moment, it felt like everything was going to be okay. Our love was strong and I believed that it could overcome any and all obstacles.

"Do you remember I told you that I had a surprise for you?" I had forgotten, but I nodded. "Come with me." He took my hand and led me outside. As we walked toward the entrance of the campus he turned to me and said: " I went to Boston and met your mom. She is amazing, Hannah."

Taken aback, I asked: "What... why..." He continued walking, still holding my hand. As we stepped into the garden at the entrance of the campus, I noticed fairy lights draping the area, tea light candles floating in the water fountain, and grey steel buckets filled with red roses scattered across the grass. There were students gathered around the garden, probably just as confused and curious as I was. Disoriented, I turned to him for answers.

"I went to Boston to ask your mom if I could make her daughter my wife." He explained and pulled a diamond ring out of his pants' pocket and held it out to me. Out of the corner of my eye, I saw someone approaching and almost fainted when I realized it was Alex.

"Hannah!" he called out. With every step he came closer, my heart raced more until he was hugging me. At that moment, I knew he was there because he wanted us to get back together, but I also knew that our timing was off. I knew that if he settled down for me, he'd be settling for less than he deserved, less than he wanted from life.

So, before he could speak, I whispered in his ear: "It'll always be you, always..."

I pulled away from him, turned back to Eric, smiled, and said: "Yes... Of course, I'll marry you."

The End

I dedicate this book to my dear friend, Helen.
Thank you for having faith in me when I didn't have faith in myself.

Don't miss out!

Visit the website below and you can sign up to receive emails whenever Samantha Snyman publishes a new book. There's no charge and no obligation.

https://books2read.com/r/B-A-UECXB-NTNDF

BOOKS2READ

Connecting independent readers to independent writers.

About the Author

Samantha is an aspiring writer with a passion for storytelling. While new to the world of writing, she is eager to explore her creativity and share her unique voice with the world.

With a love for words and a desire to create captivating narratives, Samantha is embarking on an exciting journey into the world of storytelling. When not penning her thoughts onto paper, she can be found daydreaming about her next plot twist, drowning herself in books for inspiration, or spending time with family and friends.

With a heart filled with aspiration and a mind furnished with endless ideas, Samantha is thrilled to take her first steps as a writer and bring her stories to life for readers to enjoy.